Journey to Utah

Journey to Utah

FRANK RODERUS

DOUBLEDAY & COMPANY, INC.

GARDEN CITY, NEW YORK

1977

All of the characters in this book are fictitious, and
any resemblance to actual persons, living or dead, is
purely coincidental.

Library of Congress Cataloging in Publication Data

Roderus, Frank.
Journey to Utah.

I. Title.
PZ4.R688Jo [PS3568.O346] 813'.5'4
ISBN: 0-385-13003-1
Library of Congress Catalog Card Number 76-57867

Journey to Utah

CHAPTER 1

When the girl saw me she gave out a choked little yelp of surprise and her eyes went wide like she was scared half to death. She had been bending over the fire with a tin-can boiling pot in one hand and a smaller tin-can cup in the other. I guess she'd been about to pour herself a cup of something, but she never. She stayed just the way she was, stooped over and eyes fastened on me, and even with it being so dark except for the shifting firelight I could see that most every bit of color had drained out of her face. That girl was scared.

Now I will be the first to say that I ain't the handsomest man that ever was. You could even say that I don't all fit together just right, having arms that look too long and shoulders too wide and legs that are way too short for the rest of me. My shoulders and arms are lumpy from so many hours digging water tanks and irrigation ditches when I was a kid. And my legs are bowed from sitting a saddle until they look, well, stumpy. Which is how I got my name. Stumpy. It is really James Denton Williams, but I don't believe anyone has called me that in fifteen years, not since I was nineteen or thereabouts. Anyway, what I started out to say was that I had not before been accused of actually frightening women or small children with my homeliness. They might of peered at me close a second or third time, but they never acted that dead-serious scared before.

It seemed a special shame now because this was one pretty girl I had gone and got upset. She had dark eyes set wide, astraddle of a pert little tip-turned-up nose, and her skin was fair complected over delicate bones in an oval shape. Her cheeks looked soft as a newborn filly's muzzle, of which nothing could be softer, and while right now her mouth was drawn down into a tight little button with strain lines at the corners, you could see how round and gentle her lips would normally set. She must have been ready to retire for the night because her hair had been let down. It was black. Long and thick and blacker than the night and just then it was somewhat tangled. That puzzled me, too, for she did not look to be the kind who would leave her hair untended. She had a look of quality about her as if she was used to being tidy.

Once I noticed that about her hair I began noticing other things too. She was built trim, near to being skinny in fact, and she was dressed for being out of doors. She was wearing a light brown shirtwaist that I now could see was no longer crisp and showed a smudge here and there. She had on a long brown riding skirt and good, lace-up riding boots. The skirt was of some heavy material and it was not tore but did show plenty of dust, and the boots were terrible scuffed and scratched.

It began to get through to me that mayhap she had good reason to be scared out here in the dark.

"Evenin', missus," I said, not knowing just how to address her. I guess I forgot to mention that she looked on the young side of marrying age yet, maybe sixteen or thereabouts, but a fellow never knows. For all I could tell she might of had three kids and been widowed already. "Hope I didn't startle you none."

She straightened up and cast her eyes to left and right behind me, but there wasn't anything there to be seen. When she looked back on my face she forced a be-polite-to-company smile that didn't rest easy on her lips. They quivered just a bit like they would have preferred a different expression, but she would not allow it. "Just a little," she said.

"Didn't mean to do that, ma'am. I'm sorry," I said. "I had no idea there was a lady here. It's been a long day, and when I seen your fire here I thought I might find company for the night. Didn't mean to intrude."

I gathered my reins and would have turned to go but I was stopped by something in her eyes. My gosh, if she had been scared when I first come up she was purely terrified now. I knew it was not the right thing to do without some sign of invitation, but I could not help myself. I swung down off my saddle and went over in front of her.

"Ma'am? Are you all right, ma'am?"

She got control of herself. You could see in her eyes the moment she reached back into herself with raw nerve and got things back under control. She gave a little flip of the head that set her hair to dancing in the firelight and pushed that bit of a smile back in place. It had got lost for a while there. "Of course," she said. "Of course I am all right, thank you."

I would have turned back to my horse and got out of there as was proper, but I could see she wanted to ask something. Three times her lips began to part before she got it out. She made it sound casual and offhand when she did it, like it was nothing of any importance.

"You say you were passing by and saw my fire?"

"Yes, ma'am," I said. "But don't worry. It's a common enough thing for folks to share a fire. It don't mean anything."

I thought that might reassure her, seeing as she was alone out here. Come to think of it, what *was* she doing out alone in empty country? Not that it was any of my never-mind. But it did not reassure her of anything. Her eyes got a hint wider and her lips a hint tighter but she kept herself in hand.

"Oh, I know that," she said. "I was merely surprised that you could see the fire." Again she made it sound like just polite conversation between strangers. But it meant something to her, sure enough, so I thought it might be best to explain it to her.

Now maybe I should mention that this camp I had wandered into was set down at the bottom of a dry wash, not really a good place to settle for the night but reasonably safe in late summer like this was, when there wouldn't be quite so much danger of a far-off storm filling the wash bank to bank with water. Most folks know better than to camp in a wash no matter how dry the bottom, but some never do learn and some of them are drowned. I guess they never stop to think that a wash has to be dug by water. Lots of water. And you never know for sure when it is coming. Anyway this girl had put her fire at the bottom of a slope-sided old wash and must have thought she had it hid from view.

"Why, it can be seen real easy, ma'am," I said. I pointed to the bank off behind her fire. "You see that rise there?" She nodded. "Well now, it is higher than the other side, see? An' right up there toward the top you can prob'ly see how this here bank sort of steepens up an' ends in a little overhang. See it there?" She nodded again, and her expression had gone slack. That was a curious thing and I should have took warning from it, but I did not. I went on talking. "That there overhang picks up the firelight and reflects it out just the same as the back of a tin lantern, ma'am. You can see it for miles."

I smiled at her. I guess I wanted to assure her that everything was chugging right along with the laws of nature or some such, but I needn't have bothered. Just then she wasn't seeing me nor anything or anybody else on the outside of her own skull.

That pretty girl's eyes begun to roll back in her head, and her lips was drawn back as if to snarl over teeth that were clacking together. Her limbs shook and jerked, and she let out with a low, growling moan that at first sounded so much like a cornered lynx that I started to look around for one. Then I realized it was coming from her.

Lordy, I didn't know what to do. This pretty thing was all set to turn into a genuine crazy person, and me standing right there in front of her.

I never had time to think about what I could do or should do or would do. I reacted without thinking on it, the same as a body will if he grabs hold of a piece of iron just off the forge. What I did was to grab her by the arms and shake her, hard, the same as if she was a man.

Maybe it was no way to treat a lady, but it seemed to work. Her teeth kept a-chattering, but her eyes started to come down out of her head and pretty soon she had control over her limbs again.

She sagged like she felt awful weak, but as soon as she was looking at me and really *seeing* that I was there I turned loose of her quick.

"I ain't trying to get fresh with you, ma'am, honest, but you need some help."

She nodded, and I felt better about it. She was so weak she was swaying from side to side and there was beads of sweat—perspiration—above her upper lip, but she looked to be herself again. She gathered herself together and said, "Put the fire out." It was no louder than a whisper, but her voice didn't break. This girl had more nerve than it might have seemed.

"You're on the dodge from somebody, ma'am," I said, and it was no question the way I put it to her. She nodded but didn't say anything.

"If you will take my advice then, I will leave that fire alone. I seen it for a full half hour before I got here. Anyone else out there has likely seen it too by now, so putting it out wouldn't do you no good. Now, where's your horse?"

"I . . . I don't have one," she said. That surely explained why I had not seen nor heard it since I rode up, but it did make things curiouser and curiouser.

Another thought came to me and I asked, "Where's your gear? Food? Water? Do you have anything at all?"

She shrugged and looked down at her hands. She was still holding the two tin cans, one big one and a little one, but now there was only a mess of wet leaves in the bottom of the big one and nothing at all in the little one. There was a big wet splotch on the side of her skirt. It was already drying.

"I'm sorry," she said. "I am afraid I cannot offer you a cup of tea now." There was a twitch at the corners of her mouth when she said it, not enough to be a smile but it was real. In the middle of whatever this was, she could still be amused by making herself the butt of a small joke.

"You settle yourself beside that clump of brush over there, ma'am," I said. "Does anyone come I will hear them an' give you the word. If that happens I want you to crawl smack into them bushes an' lay still. No matter what happens, you lay still. Even if you just absolutely *know* that you've been seen. Even if someone *tells* you they can see you. Lay still."

This girl might be awful scared but her brain was working all right again. "Why?"

"Because that's one of the easiest ways there is to find someone who's doing a good job of staying hid. Tell them you can see them and will shoot if they don't stand up in plain sight right away. The only trick for the fella holding the gun is to remember he shouldn't be waving it in all directions. If he remembers that, he can make it look and sound for real."

"Oh." She sat where I had pointed. "You make it sound like you know something about this sort of thing." She drew her knees up and wrapped her arms around them. She was mostly in shadow there, but she looked to be interested and intent rather than jumpy like she had been before.

"Yes, ma'am," I said. I pulled the kak off my horse and left it on the ground while I led the miserable beast off about fifty yards and hobbled it. If someone came up to the fire it wouldn't do to have a horse so close it was obvious it had just been turned loose. That horse was maybe the ugliest, square-headed animal I had ever laid eyes on and so stupid it couldn't find grass if it wasn't standing on it. So timid it would spook at a rock just on the notion the thing *might* jump at him and so slow you started back to the wagon for dinner as soon as you'd had breakfast. Still, he didn't know the meaning of quit, and I was used to him so I scratched him behind the ears a little and then went back to the fire. The girl was sitting where I'd left her.

I laid my things out around the fire and told her, "If you're interested I have a little coffee here and the makings for pan bread and bacon." She didn't say anything, but when the meal was ready she ate her share of it or a little bit more. She was dainty about her eating but she didn't let that stop her from packing it away. I wondered how long it had been since her last meal, but she never said anything about it one way or another.

We were finished with the supper and I had everything stowed back in its place before I heard company coming.

"Best get back in the brush now, ma'am," I said in a low tone. She didn't argue nor ask why she should, and the next time I looked that way I could see nothing but sand and rock and brush. It seemed she might not know too much but she was a quick one to learn, and that is a rare thing.

Out in the darkness I could hear horses coming close, at least three and maybe as many as five of them. I cannot pretend to judge better than that from the sound alone, especially as they were taking care not to make noise. Then my horse snorted. I couldn't see him, but I knew his head would be lifted and his ears forward and he prob'ly had some tag ends of grass sticking out the corners of his mouth. I had to chuckle, thinking of the sight of the dumb thing. Had to wonder what those fellas out in the dark were making of the sound of him, too. They wouldn't have been expecting that.

They did like I'd half expected them to after they heard a beast where they had not expected one. They quit pussyfooting around out there and rode up to the fire. Three of them, there was.

They were tall fellows, all cut from the same mold and well mounted on grain-fed horses that had bright hair and a layer of fat under the skin. There was no wild Barb in the blood of these horses. They looked more like a cross maybe between Thoroughbred and Cleveland Bay like some boys up to Wyoming had been playing with. Not a bad cross except they had been trying to get big, strong horses that had some cow sense in their heads, and they did not do it. The cow sense got left out, which is understandable since neither side of the family had any of it to start with. What they got, mostly, was big horses good to look at, with long legs and heavy bone.

The men that was riding them had something of the same look about them. Big boys, they were, and good-looking. Clean-shaven. Square jaws. Light brown hair curling out from under their hats. They were dressed better than cowpunchers. You'd expect to see their like behind a bank window or bossing a land development survey crew. Or mayhap just raising the Old Ned and going back to Daddy's big house for sleeping purposes from time to time. My, I couldn't hold a candle to such bully gents as these.

They sat their horses at the edge of the firelight where I could see them until I issued the invitation they'd been waiting for. "Light and set," I told them. "Supper's over, but if you have some water I'll supply the pot an' the coffee grounds."

The nearest one to me gave me a grin the like of which would warm a mother's heart. Especially if that mother had an unmarried daughter. "Obliged," he said, and the three of them swung down. From the way they stretched and stamped you could tell they had been out of contact with the ground for a good many hours.

They pulled their gear off their horses, hobbled and loosed them, and I cocked an eyebrow at the one who seemed to be the leader of this crowd.

"Say now," he said, "maybe we've gone too far." He gave me another boyish grin as disarming as a Hindoo charming a snake. "Tom," he said to one of the others, "you stake those ponies where we can get to them. We'll set up our own camps on down a ways."

The boy turned back to me and touched the brim of his hat, a fine thing of brown fur felt. My hat was made of wool felt and tended to droop around the edges unless I pinned the brim up with a thorn. "I'm Ben Trask," he said. "That's my brother Leo. And Tom with the horses."

"Pleased to meet you fellas," I said, and introduced myself, since I got the idea they would expect it, wherever they were from.

Leo fetched a water bag from among their gear, and we proceeded to boil up some coffee. When he brought it the bag was full and I took a taste of it before it went into the boiling pot. If I hadn't already known there was something wrong with these fellows, that water would have me curious anyway. It still had a fresh, clean taste to it and had not been hauled around in the sun all day, yet wherever they had filled that bag they had not stopped for the night.

I laced my coffee extra heavy with sugar, the way any puncher will do, and they did the same then although Leo and Tom had already begun to drink theirs before I reached for the sugar sack.

"We're new to this country," Ben said, "else we wouldn't have made ourselves so free with your camps."

Now there was another curious thing. The first time he said it I'd let it slide by but here he was doing it again, as if he wanted me to know him and his brothers were good ole range boys even if they were in strange country. The thing is, saying camps instead of camp when you are talking about just one place is a Texas way of talking, and that one word can really stand out in a whole herd of them even when you are not trying to pay any mind to such things.

Well, I figured, if he wants me to play a little game with him I will go right along with it. "Sounds like you boys are from down Texas way," I observed.

"Why, we are for a fact," he said with an extra heavy drawl and a free and easy touch of surprise in his voice. He turned to his brothers and said, "It wouldn't pay to try an' hide anything from this 'poke," and they smiled and shook their heads in rapt wonder at how quick I'd caught onto them.

My oh my, but this was starting to be fun. That boy Ben was laughing up his sleeve at poor dumb Stumpy so hard I was feared he might choke.

Now I will admit that I ain't particular bright. I've lost my silver to the shell game man a time or two, and when I was young and foolish I've blowed my wad on mining shares. But Lordy, if you're going to trap a coyote, do it on your own range, not his. These boys was having a high old time making a fool of this dumb puncher, talking Texas and riding Wyoming horses and setting Montana style saddles that were single rigged like they do up there in dally roping country. Texas boys tie fast to the horn and ride double-rigged saddles. Not that I expected these boys to do either one. By way of working a rope, that is.

Ben got down to the point of our little palaver then, and it was about time. They had used up enough of my coffee and sugar with their fooling around. "Say, Stumpy, maybe you can help us. We're out here looking for our little sister. She's gone and got herself lost."

He went on to tell me a long story about how their baby sister had been staying at the ranch of some kin—unnamed in his tale— and had wandered off and got lost and now her three big brothers were just desperate to find her before she got herself hurt out here by her lonesome. "If you've seen any sign of her we'd sure appreciate knowin' it," Ben said.

I pretended to give that some thought and then shook my head. "No-o-o-o, not as I recollect. The last tracks I seen was early this

morning, and I'd be willing to swear they was made by Windy
Morgan's old grulla. Everything else I crossed today was running
barefoot and in bunches and was sure to be wild horses or else
breeding bands turned loose with a colt crop. Didn't see anything
else that was shod."

Now actually, if there is such a fella as this Windy Morgan I've
never met him nor heard of him, and if he rides an old grulla it
would be an interesting happenstance. But I thought it sounded
good. The truth is, I was just passing through myself on my way
to Utah and didn't know the name of anyone in fifty mile, any direction.

"I reckon I forgot to mention the most important thing,
Stumpy. This sister of ours is afoot," Ben drawled in his very best,
grade-A, south Texas drawl. "That's one reason we're so scared for
her. We came up on her horse yesterday. Had to shoot it."

Humpf. He forgot to mention that, my left earlobe. I had to
give him credit for a nice try, though, and it hadn't cost him nothing. It could have worked.

"Now that's a different story entire, ain't it? No, Ben, I know
I've seen no foot tracks of any sort. Shucks, if I had she would've
been found an' safe by now." I was starting to gild the lily overmuch now, but I wasn't bright enough to see it at the time. "I
can promise you if I come upon her tomorrow I'll see her home
safe, boys. Dang me if I don't."

"We shorely 'preciate that," my friend Benjamin said, although
his brothers looked some worried. "What you could do is, if you
find her you can fire three shots as a signal. We found her tracks
today so if you see her at all it should be close around here, and
we'd be able to hear." He paused and looked kind of embarrassed.
He really was very good at it and might have sold me some more
mining shares had we been on his home territory. "There's just
one thing we should tell you, Stumpy. Our sister . . . Well, she
. . . she hasn't been real well. That's why she's been staying with
our uncle, see. If you find her maybe you could just call us and
we'll take her home ourselves. A stranger might . . . upset her
. . . more than she should be." His little pauses strung the words
out to quite a complete story.

I was wondering how the girl was taking this. I'd been having so much fun with our little talk that I had most forgot she was laying there in the brush and could prob'ly hear every word that was said. I'll just bet she was mad enough to spit.

Anyway, I nodded, just as serious as I could, to show I understood. "I'll do what I can, boys. I promise you that. But, say, if I find her I'll have to send up a smoke. As you can see from looking, I ain't heeled."

"You don't have a gun in your sack?" It was Leo that asked. That nice young boy seemed considerable brightened by the thought. I don't think Ben would have let it show. Nor did he, for that matter.

"You see what I'm wearin'," says I. "Used to have a belly gun but I lost it somewheres a while back and never got around to getting another. Don't really need one as long as I've got that square-headed old cayuse out there." I pointed my chin off into the darkness where my horse was tearing at what little grass could be found there.

Leo grunted and I saw that Ben gave him a dark, shut-up sort of look, which he did.

Ben prob'ly knew that about the only reason a working cowhand carries a gun is to shoot his own horse if he loses his seat and finds himself with a foot caught in a stirrup. Then it is shoot and walk or maybe get drug to death. He uses a gun for that or maybe to make noise with when he goes to town. Most gunfights take place in penny dreadfuls or on a stage. Not all, of course, but most of them when you get right down to the facts of it. Anyhow, Ben should have known that, and if he did not I was not going to make him start wondering by explaining things to him. After all, I knew him and his brothers to be rough and ready ole boys from down Texas way, didn't I?

Ben thanked me most politely and allowed that while they searched in the morning they would keep an eye out for my smoke. Just in case. Then he thanked me again, for the coffee this time, while his brothers put their horses under saddle and those good old Texas boys sloped out of there and down the wash.

I listened to their progress as long as I could and then whispered, "Stay hid" to the girl before I slipped along behind them on foot for a ways to make sure they did not double back unexpected. They went about a mile down the wash before they set up their camp and rolled into their blankets for the night. A good hard rain up-country would be too much to ask for, I thought on the way back, but a body can always hope.

On the way back to the fire I gathered up my horse. He was saddled and ready to go before I called to the girl. "All right, ma'am. You can come out now."

I waited but she didn't show. That patch of brush looked empty.

"Lady, you can come out now."

Still nothing.

"Lady?" My gosh, what if she was gone? What if she'd slipped off somewheres while I was away? Those fellas'd be sure to find her the next day. "Ma'am?"

I was commencing to get worried about her. I eased into that patch of brush, thinking to see if I could find some sign of which way she had gone. Instead I stepped plumb on her.

"Ouch." She rolled out from under my boot and I couldn't have been more startled if I'd stepped on a rattlesnake.

"Well fer cryin' out loud, lady. Why'dn't you come when I called you?"

She was sitting in the middle of that dry, brittle growth brushing off her clothes from where she'd been laying on the ground. And from where I had stomped on her too, most likely.

"You *said* for me to be still no matter *what* happened. That is precisely what I was doing."

"Yes, ma'am." She raised a hand to me and I pulled her to her feet, maybe a bit rougher than was needed.

She did some more brushing and fussed at her hair some with the tips of her fingers. Then she seemed to give up on that. She shrugged and tossed her head so that the long hair flowed down her back and out of her way. She smiled at me and asked, "What do you think of my brothers?"

"Them fellows really are your brothers, ma'am?"

"Sort of," she said, cocking her head to one side. "Their mother

and my father are married, so you could say they are my brothers.
I wouldn't say it, but you could. They do tell a plausible story,
don't they?"

"Yes, ma'am. They do."

"And?"

"And what, ma'am?"

"I heard what they told you. You have no reason to doubt
them. Are you going to take me back to my sweet, likeable
brothers?"

"Ma'am, those boys are likeable enough. Why, that Ben's smile
would melt a candle. But I reckon I will not take you back to
them against your will."

"Even though I might be . . . I believe Ben inferred that I was
'ill.'"

"Ma'am, I don't know a thing about crazy people. For all I
know, the only reason you ain't swinging from branch to branch
in the trees is because there aren't any trees around here. I will
give you an opinion on that when we get into some woods. In the
meantime I will just trust my own judgment. And that says for
you and me to get out of here. Right now."

"All right, Mr. Williams. Thank you."

"You are welcome, ma'am. An' the name is Stumpy. My daddy
never named me Mister or he would have told me about it."

"Very well, Mr. Stumpy Williams." She peered up at me past a
hank of hair that had slipped forward. She really was a tiny thing,
though I hadn't noticed it so much until she was up close like
that. "What is your proper name?" she asked, so I told her. Then
she said, "I am Janet Cates. NOT Trask, thank goodness. And if
you are ready, we can leave now."

"Yes'm, Miss Janet Not-Trask Cates."

I bundled her aboard that old horse of mine, and she sat him
astraddle, like a man, without a word of comment. Even wearing
a riding skirt like she was, the hem of her skirt rode up near to her
boot tops. I put that out of my mind but quick and gathered up
the reins in my hand. Then I happened to remember something
and turned back toward my saddlebags.

"Excuse me, Miss Janet," I said. I pulled my gunbelt and old .44-40 Remington out of there and strapped them on.

"I thought you said you had no gun, Mr. Williams."

"Yes, ma'am. I reckon you have caught me out in a lie, Miss Janet. But I don't usually calculate to need a gun real sudden unless I'm among folks, ma'am, and until just recent there was just me and this horse to think about."

"My brothers wear their guns at all times."

"Yes, ma'am, but they are a mite younger than me. The darn things get heavy, Miss Janet. You don't see a carpenter with his box of tools in his hand all the time nor a cowhand all cluttered up with ropes and irons day in and day out either."

"The tools of your trade, Mr. Williams?"

"That is not exactly what I said, ma'am, and I would not want you raising any hopes about me goin' and shooting up your brothers for you."

"And that is not at all what I asked, Mr. Williams."

"Just so we understand each other, ma'am."

"We do," she said. Said it rather primly too.

I took up the horse's reins again and commenced walking. I wanted to put a goodly number of miles between us and that still burning campfire before daylight.

CHAPTER 2

The dawning was a rose-colored explosion, it seemed like. For a long while we had been moving through the thin gray light that comes before sunrise and leads you to think you can see pretty well. Then the sun came up and all of a sudden the world turned from a gray and black woodcut print into a full color drawing.

We were into the foothills by then and back behind us could see the flat—or near flat—country we just left. In midday that dry, empty country looks about as flat as a homemade tabletop. Gouged and dented here and there but mostly flat. With the new-risen sun pouring red and orange across at a low angle, you could see that it wasn't at all flat. Instead it was as lumpy as a trail cook's gravy.

The bare tops of small rises were pointed up with a rose-tinted tan, and each little clump of grass and brush—dry and brittle this time of year—came alive with a golden yellow glow from the light behind them. Deep folds in the ground that were still hidden from the light were shown in shades of violet that deepened to a rich purple in the lowest spots.

Overhead the sky was clear, with not the first scrap of cloud nor even a hawk or eagle to catch the eye as far as you could see. Out to the east the sun was cherry red, and all around it the sky was white as skim milk. Closer toward us it commenced to turn blue. Pale at first and then richer and darker shades until behind us, off toward the west and the mountains, it was a dark blue-black.

Pretty it was, and the both of us watched it while we took a breather.

We hadn't spoke much during the night. Most of the while the girl had sat half dozing with both her small hands folded on the horn of my saddle. For nearly an hour now she had been walking, saving the horse's strength. Not that he was worth saving, but still . . . She had walked alongside of him right brisk and never offered a word of complaint, though I could see she was starting to tucker. I had showed her to hang onto the stirrup leathers with one hand while she walked, being as she was too little to hold onto the horn comfortably. That may seem like mighty little assistance, that tiny bit of pull while a horse walks beside you, but it is nothing to the horse and can add miles to a human person's stamina. Seems odd, but it works and can be a handy thing to know.

The wind picked up with the dawning. The air had been cool but nearly dead still through the night. Now there were quick, hard puffs of wind that soon would turn into a steady, day-long push. It is a funny thing about that dry, steady wind. On the one hand it sweeps over the land sucking every scrap of moisture from rock, leaf, or living thing. At the same time, it drives those rattling, clanking, blessed windmills that pump water and so make the empty land useful for cattle or other livestock. The same wind robs you of water one way and gives it back in another. It is enough to make a body think.

I jammed my old hat tighter on my head and turned toward the girl. "Time we get along now, Miss Janet."

She came back from whatever distant place she had been seeing and gave me a small smile. The sun was in her face, pulling her eyes tight at the corners, and her skin was slack with fatigue. It had been a long night. The harsh, direct light could find no roughness in the texture of that skin, though. My, but she was a young and pretty thing. She took hold of a stirrup leather and waited for me to lead the horse off.

"You can go ahead an' ride, ma'am, no farther than we're going just now."

She mounted without waiting for me to give her a hand up. Understandable enough as she was alone with a stranger in rough country. I reminded myself to keep my distance. There was no need of her being scared of me too.

"Are we close to our destination?" she asked when she was settled in the saddle.

"I expect so, ma'am. For a few hours anyway. The horse could use a drink and a little rest."

"I imagine you could use a rest too, Mr. Williams. It is good you know this area."

Now I reckoned it was mighty considerate of her to be thinking of me when she had so many troubles of her own. "I wisht I did know this country, ma'am, but I think we can find some water soon."

She peered around. We were about halfway up a long slope leading to some tall benches. Beyond them should be either an easy plateau or possibly some real cut-up rough country. From where we were we could only see the brush- and rock-dotted slope and the rock-walled bench at the top. "I don't see any trees or green grass," she said. "Do you think you can really find water here?"

"Should be, ma'am. There was some quail talking up there just before the sun come up, and a flight of dove have been up there and gone since we stopped. Don't know how much but there should be water somewhere along that rock face."

The girl nodded. She didn't say anything but you could tell she would be tucking that information away in her head. Next time, if there was one, she would be watching for such things herself.

I took the reins of the horse and led him up the slope, the sun warm on my back and growing steady hotter. The wind did nothing to cut that heat, and later in the day it would be like a load of coals being carried on one's back and shoulders. For the moment it felt good. The climb pulled at my legs, and I would have had to admit to being some tired. The upper part of my legs felt like they were packed in a lead casing, and the short stop we had made was enough to allow sharp twinges to go shooting through my feet and up my calves for the first few hundred yards of the climb.

The slope was longer than it appeared, and it took the better part of an hour to reach the tumbled rocks at the foot of the face. It took another fifteen or twenty minutes walking along the face to the southwest before a wide hint of quail-tracked path pointed the way to a shallow rock basin where some stagnant but cool water had collected. Some brush and large rocks protected the basin from sun and wind to cut down on the evaporation. There must have been some seepage from the bench or the pool could not long remain, but it must have been a slow seep. The water was dead and flat to the taste when I knelt beside it, but it would do. I turned back toward the girl and the horse.

She slid lightly out of the saddle and leaned against the horse, wiping at her forehead with the back of her hand. It was already mighty hot. "Is there anything I can do?" she asked.

"Yes, ma'am," I said, rising. "That beast won't be able to reach the water here. Why don't you drink what you want from the canteen an' then I can water him from it."

She nodded and lifted the canteen strap over the horn. She unscrewed the cap and took a couple healthy swallows, then held the blanket-sided round canteen toward me. "Better fill up as much as you can," I told her. "The next filling won't be near so good tasting."

She did as she was told and drank until the canteen was near empty. I filled it at the basin and carried it the few steps to the horse.

That ugly thing had been in hot, dry country before. He could drink from a canteen without hardly spilling a drop and had learned to not crush the rim of the opening too. It had taken us several canteens and a goodly many smacks in the jaw for him to learn that. I held it up for him to drink the first half gallon, and the girl stood watching. "I never saw a horse do a thing like that before," she said.

"They do learn, ma'am."

I had to fill that little canteen six more times before he lost interest, then near about drained it myself and filled it again before I hung it back on the horn. The girl watched me all the while, and she got a queer sort of expression when I drunk from the canteen.

"Something wrong, Miss Janet?"

She gave a wiggly little shiver and made a face. "Ugh. That is horrible. Why didn't you drink first, at the very least? Or wash it or something?"

"As a matter of fact I wasn't sure there would be enough for all three of us in this little seep. And anyway, him an' me been sharing a jug for some time now without one of us makin' the other sick." I couldn't help adding, careful to keep from grinning, "Besides which, you drunk after him too, except by a little longer. Wouldn't of seemed proper to wash it off just for myself."

"Oh." Her eyes was wide and her lips puckered in on themselves a bit. By the time I had half turned away she was scrubbing at her mouth with her fingers but, shoot, they were dirtier than that ugly old horse of mine.

Up higher like we then was you could see quite a ways back and so I took a good, long look. Not finding anything of much interest I slipped the cinches until they were hanging loose, and told her, "We'll look for a place to rest now, ma'am."

She looked a bit uncomfortable yet but she said, "All right," and we wandered on slow until we found a good place to stop.

It was a nest of boulders not too far out from the rock wall that hung above us. There was some shade between the wall and the rocks, and nearby was enough browse that the horse could find a mouthful of something to eat. Unless he was too stupid to recognize it for food, in which case it would serve him right to go hungry.

I hobbled him and stripped the gear off his back and then used my hat to wipe him down some before I turned him loose. The girl made herself comfortable on the ground with a big rock for a backrest. She sat like she had the night before, with her knees drawn up and her arms wrapped around them. She peered at me from over the barrier made by her knees, and that may have made her feel a little bolder than she otherwise might. I turned the horse loose and stowed the gear in the shade before I sat down in the dust a few yards away from her.

"We don't have anything that could be eaten without cooking," I said, "unless you are a lot hungrier than I think. And it wouldn't be much of an idea to light a fire here."

"Why are you helping me?" she asked. It seemed awful far off the subject. She didn't act or sound like she was scared of me particularly, but I got the idea she was willing to get that way should I growl or start to unbutton my shirt or something. Her eyes—I had decided they were blue though so dark you could hardly tell it —were serious.

"Well now. I reckon it was because you needed help, ma'am. And anyway, you asked me to."

She gave a quick but firm little shake of her head that sent her hair skittering across both shoulders. "No, I did not," she said. She was looking at me just as solemn as could be. And come to think on it, she was right. That did throw a different sort of light on things.

"I guess . . . I guess I kinda thought you had, Miss Janet. What with one thing and another." I looked down at my hands and wondered what she must be thinking about a homely, sawed-off character that would just pack her onto a horse in the middle of the night and carry her off into the hills away from anything and anybody.

I knew what she saw when she looked at me, and it was not much. Old clothes covered with the dust of a lot of miles. Face burned dark by wind and covered with a thick stubble of beard. Hair tangled and probably none too clean. Too short legs stuffed down into boots run over at the heel. Too wide shoulders and too long arms that reminded folks of some sort of monkey. That always seemed to make people think right off that I'd have about as much brains and about as much morals as a monkey, too. Everybody always gets that idea. I can tell it in the way they look at me and, more, by the way they talk. Some of them talk to me in words like a story in a first-reader primer.

I looked at my hands and couldn't find much there to make me feel any better. Even they were not what one would expect. They were big enough, I guess, but the fingers are long and taper slightly to a rounded point, not blunt and squared off at the ends like one might expect. The truth is, they look weak. They aren't, especially, but they look weak. I lost a job because of them once when I was a kid, before I went off for schooling and was just rambling around some. Fella was making up a crew to string some fence and cut hay. He seemed pleased when I first braced him about signing on, but then he took a look at my hands, said that was the way he always judged could a man work, and told me that I wouldn't be any good on his crew. He told me with a mean kind of sneer that he'd heard there was a job open for a sheepherder but that he only wanted men on his crew. It was an odd reason for losing a job but it happened. Not that I minded all that much in the long run. The fella'd been part right anyway, and the job tending sheep on summer pasture went some longer and paid five dollars a month more than I'd have made on his crew.

Anyway, I thought about that sort of thing awhile, but I was just avoiding the issue. I really didn't know what to tell the girl. At least she seemed to think I was relatively harmless at the moment. As long as she didn't rattle my cage.

"If I have acted improperly, ma'am . . ." I said, and then ran down again.

"Not at all, Mr. Williams," she said. Even without looking at her I could tell that she felt more confident now. In her voice now there was an unmistakable tone of quality folk patronizing the serfs. And I can see that I earned it. I really must have seemed an oaf, sitting there staring at my hands and twisting at my fingers. I was half tempted to knuckle my forelock in a gesture of obeisance, but my hat would of got in the way.

"I appreciate what you have done for me," she said. "I really do. And I want you to know that. I did not mean to be rude when I corrected you, but I would not have asked anyone to put himself in danger on my account. You can understand that, can't you?" She sounded mildly hopeful but not at all certain that I could understand the finer distinctions in responsibility there. It seemed that now, in broad daylight where she could get a better and more leisurely look at me, she was afraid she was going to be saddled with the responsibility for my welfare as well as her own. But as long as I agreed that she had not specifically requested my assistance, then it was my own lookout if anything went wrong.

"Yes'm," I mumbled, rather deliberately vague. After all, she seemed to have assigned me to a level about one notch higher than the village idiot. If she was comfortable thinking that—after

I had fed her, watered her, and pulled her out of a scrap with the Brothers Trask—well, let her go on thinking it.

And all right. I admit it. I was peeved with her. She had gone and hurt my delicate little feelings. Maybe I was pouting a bit, when you get right down to it. That is neither a mature nor a rational reaction, but it is easier to judge after the fact than during it and I do have the excuse of it being a decidedly human response. So I mumbled, "Yes'm," which was nothing more than knuckling the forelock in a different manner.

We didn't do much talking after that, just sat quiet and listened to the horse chew while I watched back the way we had come. In no time at all the land took on a flat, gray-brown look that wouldn't do anything toward enticing a weary traveler.

To look at it you would think that nothing could live there that was not just passing through. Yet there had always been aplenty of wildlife there. Birds and reptiles, of course, for they can live most anywhere, but there are also the animals. Small ones like the mice and hares. Bigger ones like coyotes and the little prairie wolves, which are different animals entire, and bobcats and packs of javelina, though mostly those mean little porkers are found further to the south than where we were. There were even some big animals about, like deer and antelope and the desert breed of bighorn sheep. And now, of course, you could find cattle.

It seemed that cattle could make out in the scrub just fine as long as they had water, and a valuable discovery that was, too. For a while there people thought you couldn't do much with cows where buffalo hadn't ranged before them, but that was proved false quick enough.

Those big herds of wild buffalo were gone now. Killed off by the hide hunters and the soldiers. Profit was the reason they gave, and to put a lock on the plains Indians. Now there were cattle and farms on the grasslands, and even if the big herds could rebuild nobody would let them. The buffalo were before my time, but I saw a little band of them once over in the Palo Duro where they were penned up on the floor of that fault being protected by a man whose name I disremember. Anyway they must have been some sight when the herds ran on for miles instead of being just a few dozen spotted here and there.

What I started to say, though, was that the buffalo needed lots of grass. They never came over into this scrub country and so for a time people figured cattle would not increase here either. Now they've found that if you give enough water to a crossbred cow she will pick around the thorns and the rocks and calve just as regular as a grassland stock cow. You can't do this with fine-blooded animals, but you can cross their blood into range cattle and get a nice doing beef animal that will breed and survive and still put on pounds better than the old line of half-wild Spanish cattle that started the whole thing.

You would think from all this loose chatter that I was preparing to give a high school lecture on the subject. I suppose what I am really trying to do is put off admitting just how bad I let that girl down. It was not a thing to be proud of.

CHAPTER 3

The Trask boys were not more than a hundred yards away and coming at a fast and easy hand gallop when I saw them. They were sitting back in their big northern saddles and already had their revolvers loose in their hands. Confident, those boys were.

Well, they had every reason to be. They had caught us cold, with a sheer wall of solid rock at our backs and open space to either side. There was no place we could run even if we had time to reach that old horse of mine, which we did not in any case. I had gone and dropped off to sleep like I hadn't a care in the world.

There didn't seem to be many options open to us. We couldn't run, so all that was left was to either fight or quit. Fighting seemed an awful poor choice. It would be one gun against three, and there would always be a strong possibility that the girl would get hurt if it came to warfare. Quitting did not sound much better, but then the girl was kin to these boys. It was plain they wanted her for something. I did not know what it might be. Either most unpleasant—at best—or fatal—at the worst. Whatever it was, she had been running from them hard, so there was some powerful reason to keep her out of their hands. Powerful in her mind anyway, which might or might not be sound.

Of course I didn't take time to reason this out while those boys were racking along toward us. The facts were pretty open. They didn't take much thinking about, especially since I've never been much for gambling with somebody else's money. Or life.

"Slip around behind that rock you're leanin' against and lay down, ma'am," I said. "Make yourself as little and as low as you can get." I slipped the thong off the hammer of my revolver to free it in the holster and then scrambled to my feet.

By now the Trask boys were about fifty yards off and could see every move I made. They reined their horses to a quick stop and the one in the middle, Ben, was grinning. He surely did seem to be one happy, easygoing fella. Long as your back wasn't to him, anyway.

"I see you found her," he called over the distance that separated us. His voice was as pleasant as it had been the night before, and him with a gun in his hand. It was a thing to remember. That boy gave me the impression of a man who'd shoot someone as casual as he'd light a cigarette. I nodded to him.

"I suppose she had some wild tale to tell you," Ben called. I shook my head.

"Are you going to raise a fuss when we take her home?" Ben asked. I nodded my head again. Slow and easy, I took hold of the nicked and age-polished walnut stocks of my old Remington and hefted it out of the leather. I didn't raise it, just let it dangle like an extension of my wrist. I thought I could trust the boy to know it was not just a threat.

Ben's grin got even wider. Even at that distance I could see how his eyes must have been dancing in their imitation of happiness.

Tom and Leo started to nudge their horses out in as pretty a sidepass as you could hope to see. Just a hint of inside leg pressure on the flank and those big, handsome horses bowed their necks and began daintily moving sideways.

There is something extra pretty about that motion in a well-set-up animal. It is even prettier when they are moving forward at the same time. A really knowledgeable charro can put on a performance with a horse that would rival any ballet ever written for the sheer beauty of motion. To my mind anyway.

Those big bays hadn't moved but a couple steps out in their gun-ready fan before Ben said something to his brothers too low for me to hear. Leo looked disappointed but both boys immediately reversed their leg pressure and the bays tucked themselves back in next to Ben's horse. Oh, it was pretty. With my left hand I touched the brim of my hat to show the appreciation I felt. Ben nodded, still pleasant as could be, and the boys wheeled their horses together like they were under a single set of reins. Like I said. Pretty.

They rode back down the slope nearly a hundred yards, then Ben turned toward Leo and seemed to be telling him something. All three drew rein and Leo dismounted. He swung his horse sideways to us and stood on the far side. At first I couldn't make out what he was doing. He hadn't pulled the carbine from its boot on his saddle rigging. Then I saw a puff of smoke over his saddle. He had been using it for a rest for an accurate shot at long range. With his revolver.

I couldn't figure it. It didn't make sense. They were close to a hundred fifty yards away and shooting uphill. Anybody who says he can shoot a black powder handgun accurately at that distance is lying. And anyway it was clear that they did not want the girl dead. Otherwise why would they back off instead of opening the ball when they were sure to win, when they were close and had us three guns to one? It didn't make sense. None. I heard no slug plowing air near me and the girl—I looked quickly—was not in view.

And then it did make sense and within me there came a coldness that I had not felt in a long time. It seemed to start at the base of my skull and flood downward in a gushing fall of ice and fire. For to our right, perhaps thirty yards down the slope, my ugly, miserable old gelding coughed once—an apologetic sound, it was—and folded slowly to his knees and to the ground.

He fell heavily onto his right side, twitched violently several times and was dead. Just as slowly as he had gone down I replaced my revolver in its holster.

Far below, Leo remounted his bay. The three brothers separated, one going to either side of us downslope from the bench face and the third moving further away but staying directly below. There was no way we could possibly walk past any of the three without being exposed to fire if they chose to shoot.

Those boys were a puzzlement for sure. There was no way to tell whether they wanted to force surrender of the girl from thirst or if they regarded this as a sure means of killing us both with less danger to themselves than they would have faced in a straight-out gunfight. It could have been either way. Or something else entirely, something I was not bright enough to read from their actions.

I stood in the heat of the sun with sweat escaping from under my hatband and thought about such things as that. It was better than thinking about the horse. It was better than thinking about the Trask boys and my feelings toward them. It would not do to permit any impairment of my judgment. That would not do. Not at all.

I walked to the horse. I did not want to. But I needed to. It was a kid thing to do, I guess, but I knelt and straightened the hair of his forelock. God, he had been an ugly horse. God! Damn them. Please.

When I got up, the girl was standing there beside me. She had a queer expression, half tenderness and half disbelief. I had to blink several times, hard, before I could see her clearly.

"Why?" she asked. She was covered with dust and grime. The front of her shirtwaist and heavy skirt were soiled from her having to hide on the ground. She brushed at her hair with her fingertips.

I shrugged my shoulders. "It keeps us from running away from them." I pulled a none too clean bandanna from my hip pocket and used it to wipe the sweat from my face. Felt good, too. "Miss Janet, I . . . I don't want to sound pushy, ma'am, or anything like that. But it would surely help me to figure out what we should do if . . . well . . . if I knew a little about those boys' intentions." I hurried on. "I mean, I'm not trying to pry but you never said much beyond that those boys were after you. It would help aplenty to know if their interest in you could be . . . uh . . . fatal."

"Oh, my." She looked distressed. "I really had not thought . . . Mr. Williams, you will find this difficult to believe, but I had not actually given thought to the extent of my stepbrothers' intentions toward me. I suppose I have been so busy with evasion that their intentions simply . . . did not come to mind." She paused. Small concentration wrinkles appeared on her forehead. Somehow they made her look all the more vulnerable. She looked at me, head cocked at an angle and eyes grave. "They would be capable of anything, Mr. Williams. Absolutely anything."

"Yes, ma'am, but that don't answer my question."

"No, but . . ." The words came tumbling out now. "Mr. Williams, I do not know what their intentions are, really, and I do not know what to tell you, but I am frightened half to death and, yes, Mr. Williams, yes, they just might decide to kill us both, not just me but both of us now . . ." I cut her off with a quick gesture. It might have been rude, but that breathless rush of words was just coming too fast. I didn't want her getting wound up to the point of hysteria on me. Things were tough enough without that. And there could be no question that this little girl was under some kind of rough pressure. Even if she still was not willing to tell me what it was.

Darn it, I was commencing to get downright curious about what lay behind all this. But there was no way I could force her to tell me, and even if there had been it wouldn't have been worth the damage it would do. When you get right down to it, the only reason I wanted to know was to satisfy my own curiosity. It wouldn't help her a bit to have her problems dragged out to the view of strangers like wash on a clothesline. And the object was to help this girl. For now anyway.

I took my hat off and reset it. The fresh air underneath felt good for the brief instant it lasted. I looked at the sun and judged it to be near midafternoon. No wonder it was so powerful hot. I had no one to fault but myself for sleeping like I'd done. At least we wouldn't be in direct sun long. In another half hour the sun would move out of sight above the bench wall. It would be a relief.

I looked at the girl and saw that while she was flushed from the harsh weight of the heat, there was no sweat on her. It didn't seem natural somehow, but then what did I know about a girl such as this one?

"We'll sit and wait a while," I told her, and turned back toward the rock heap where we had been before.

She followed and we both settled on the ground with a boulder for a backrest, watching the country that was spread out below us to the east. For a time neither of us spoke. The sun moved over the high wall at our backs, and a band of cooling shadow formed and drifted lazily down the slope.

"I'm sorry about your horse," the girl said after a long silence. "It was my fault, and of course I will replace him when I am able." She would have said more but I looked at her and there was something in my expression that cut the words off and left them unsaid. She recoiled as if I had spoken all the things I had not, and I believe she was sorry for making such an offer. She was not insensitive.

There was no way, of course, that she could pay to replace that miserable beast. A horse is just an animal. A form of transportation that is not so reliable nor so fast as a train. A form of power not so strong as a steam engine or water wheel. A horse is not as smart as a dog nor half so affectionate. It can be balky. If you allow it a horse can turn on you, even kill you. Yet a good one is honest. It won't bite nor kick at you without first laying its ears back in warning. It will do your bidding time after time, day after day whether you tend it proper or don't. And after a time, after so many hours and months and years of sharing the same sunshine, the same icy storms and the same miles, there can be a sort of feeling that comes between man and beast. And I had had that feeling for that particular horse.

I could never begin to remember how many miles we had traveled together, how many nights I spent with no company save his. I had not wanted to think of these things. Not yet. But the girl's comments had loosed them and so now I sat with my back to that dry and lifeless rock and let myself think about that useful but soulless beast. And how much I would miss him if I had any future beyond this place and this day.

I thought back across the years and the travels we had shared, and there came to me many memories, like so many photographs from an Eastman camera, and now those memories were dead. The heat rose within me again, and I shoved it back to be drawn upon at a later time, when this girl would not be endangered by it.

But no, neither she nor her stepbrothers nor any other person could ever replace that horse. Those boys had gone and shot a friend of mine. One day I would explain this to them.

I shook my head, as if that would force such thoughts out of it, and the girl looked at me. When she spoke again it was on another subject, and I was grateful to her for that measure of understanding.

"Are we waiting for anything in particular, Mr. Williams?" Her eyes, seeming larger than they had before, were on mine. I may have been overreacting but at the time I wondered if she was again getting worried about having to feel responsible for my safety instead of it being the other way around. Perhaps she was just getting more worried. To be fair, we were in a bad position and I didn't seem to be doing anything more than setting on the ground and brooding.

"Yes'm, we are," I said. I paused long enough to see if she was willing to let it go at that. She surprised me by nodding her head and leaning back against the rock behind her. "What we'll have to do," I went on, "is to wait for dark and then get out of here."

"Won't they expect that?" Her curiosity was intense now.

"Yes, ma'am, they will. But I hope they won't expect what we are gonna do." I nodded to the north, east, and south. "Those boys are out there waiting for us to try and slip by. Were we foolish enough to try it they'd be all over us, prob'ly at some place they'd pick out where we couldn't get behind anything to fight back. I judge that Mr. Ben is not one to take a chance when waiting a little while might improve the odds." She nodded her agreement of that. "So what we will do is go where they ain't."

"And how do we do that?"

I grinned at her. "A man on horseback, now he gets the habit of looking for trails his horse can take. Someone afoot, though, they can climb out of places that a horse can't follow."

She twisted her head and stared up, straight up, and I watched the doubt and the worry that soon began to show on her face. Well, I knew well enough what she was seeing. I'd already looked at it myself a time or two.

The face of that wall was practically a straight fall from the top to the slope where we now sat. At first glance—second, too—it looked to be absolutely sheer for the full hundred fifty feet or so of its height. Except, of course, for some vertical clefts, like wrinkles, here and there. There could be no question about finding a trail of any kind leading up a high face like that.

The thing was, we were leaning up against proof that this bench wall was not really sheer at all. What it was was an outcropping of hard rock that was either shoved up above the place where we were sitting or had got left behind when water or wind or both tore the ground down to our level. But now and probably for a long time past that stone bench was being hacked at itself by freezing and thawing, wind and occasional rain. The loose rock, big pieces and little, at the foot proved that the bench was crumbling a little at the edges. And that rock had not been cleaved away in big, neat slabs. It had chunked off a bit here and a bit there, taking maybe a year or ten or ten thousand from one loosening tumble to the next. And every place a piece had broken out was a potential handhold or pathway for someone determined to claw his way to the top. Or hers.

"Do you really think we can do it? It is so . . . frightening, really."

"Yes, ma'am, I do." The words were yes, but at the same time I was shaking my head no. It might have been a farfetched worry, but the girl was pretty obviously examining that wall. It was just possible that young Benjamin Trask owned him a pair of field glasses.

The girl brought her eyes down from the heights even if she did leave her thoughts up there. "I've never done any climbing," she said.

"Why, neither have I, ma'am," I told her, cheerful as I could manage, "but I don't reckon it will be as hard as it looks. But say now, I'm getting mighty hungry. And there's sure no worry now about those boys finding us. Why don't I put us together a real nice fire and see can we make a meal?"

She smiled, seemed grateful for the change of a worrisome subject. "That is something I can do, Mr. Williams," she said. "If you will attend to the fire, I will do the cooking."

"That's a deal, ma'am." I got to my feet and went wood-hunting.

I soon had a small fire adding to the heat of the day, and the girl went to busying around with the little food that remained in my sack. She seemed to be having a fine time, everything considered, as she moved things on and off the fire, managing to stir up a flare of bright flame or a dust devil of ashes from time to time. I *think* she was making us biscuits and stew, though it was some hard to tell, both right off and also later when we went to eat of it.

What she came up with were some round little knobs of dough fried hard on the outside and sort of soggy in the middle and in my other pan some near raw bacon surrounded by wet, uncooked rice. It was a real unusual experience, but I smacked my lips and cleaned up every bite and asked for seconds. When I did, I held my plate out and looked at her—I hadn't before, on purpose of cowardice—and there she sat, looking square at me with quiet laugh wrinkles crinkled at the corners of her eyes.

"Mr. Williams, I must say that a man could not hope to be more polite than that." She chuckled, a soft and furry sound deep in her throat that was directed at herself. "And a woman could not be proven more wrong. I . . . uh, find that an open campfire is not quite the same as a properly stoked range when it comes to cooking."

"No, ma'am," I said. "It is not, for a fact."

CHAPTER 4

The climb, when darkness finally came, was more frustrating than it was either trying or dangerous. Although I suppose the girl might have been some scared. If she was she never mentioned it.

I took along the sack that held what was left of our food. That and the canteen fresh filled with water from the same seep we had used before. I thought about filling the pool with sand once the canteen was full, but that wouldn't have been right. Someone might have really needed that water long after its loss would have annoyed the Trask boys. I really wanted to take my saddle, too— not that it was worth so much—but that would have been a lot of extra weight that maybe I couldn't manage while we climbed. And I had to be ready to help the girl should she have need.

When it came to it, though, I needn't have worried overmuch about that. I had to give her credit. She never fussed and was no more bother than you would expect, climbing a strange place in the dark. The times she did go to slip she never called out for help or anything but tried her best to make it on her own.

The frustrating part of it all was that it was so darn hard to find a way to the top.

I had studied on that wall nearly the whole afternoon until I thought sure I had found a path clean up the face. I had it all down to memory, too, but I sure was wrong.

We hadn't more than got a good start, soon after full dark, when we got turned away from the path I'd chosen.

The first part was downright easy. Right at the back of this little niche I'd picked there was a pile of loose dirt and rock maybe thirty feet high. Figure it out. That was a fifth of the way up and gentle enough we could practically walk up it.

The only trouble was, when we got to the top of this loose stuff I couldn't quite reach the bottom of a cleft above it. I guess most of that loose rock came out of there to start with, but the drift fell short of the gap it came from.

From the ground it had looked close enough that I could climb up in there and then help the girl up. It turned out to be about ten feet from the nearest foothold to the opening of that gap. Had there been two men trying to get up there it would have been no problem. One of us could have crawled right up the other to reach a good hold and then we could have gone right up to the top. But you can't hardly do such a thing with a girl to watch out for. For the longest time I stood there like some kind of dummy, staring up at the bottom of that gap that was so close but just, just a little too far away.

I thought about it and thought about it and there must have been a dozen things I might have tried if I'd been alone even. But I kept thinking, what if I took a fall and busted a leg or something. If that happened the girl would be as good as caught by those good ole boys who called themselves her brothers. She wouldn't have a speck of a chance. Eventually I just turned and slithered back down the little distance we had gained, the girl trailing along behind.

"What do we do now?" she asked. I couldn't help but notice that now, in the dark and with something going forward, her voice was soft but accepting. She seemed not to be having many doubts about dumb old Stumpy Williams right then. But then maybe I was doing the girl a disservice right along. Maybe I just got so wound up about that at some times that I'm oversensitive about it at other times. I'm not in any position to judge that too well.

Anyway, I told her right out where it was that we stood. "I don't rightly know, Miss Janet, except that we keep looking. It seems I wasted a lot of time when I planned our route this afternoon."

"All right, Mr. Williams. Go ahead. Wherever you go, I'll be one step behind." The light was none too good, but I could see that she tossed her head a little for emphasis. This was one determined girl. For a fact.

Now I have to say it. I was not too farsighted earlier that afternoon. I had got so carried away with planning out this wonderful first path I found that I never bothered to plan out a second path just in case. Well, now it was just-in-case time. I started hiking along the bench face with the girl, just as she had said, right behind.

Thank goodness the cloudless sky we had had all day continued into the night. There was little enough light. The moon would not rise for hours. But at least there was some visibility. Cloud cover would have made it impossible to see anything.

Oh, we did climb. We climbed up. We climbed back down. And up. And down again. I honestly don't remember how many false starts we made. And I don't know about the girl, but I was getting darn tired by the time we hit that last one. The one that finally worked.

It is just a good thing that when we found that crumbling gap —it had been out of view from where we spent the afternoon—it was purely easy to get up. We never even had to do any hard climbing. Just hands and knees scrambling.

I kept looking back at the girl. She must have been having a tough time of it in that long skirt. I know I'd have tumbled down a dozen times if I'd had all that cloth wrapped around my legs. But she never fell and she never complained. It was too dark for me to see her expression though I would have liked to. For curiosity, sort of.

When we finally were standing on top of that bench I'll tell you, I was dragged out and worn down. The girl must have been too. But it sure felt good to be there. The girl slumped down to the ground. By this time she wasn't making any attempt to be careful of her skirt.

"Whew," she said. She lifted the hair off the back of her neck like even that had gotten too heavy for comfort. "That was quite a jaunt. I hope we will not have to do any more of that soon."

"No, ma'am. I don't expect so."

She let her hair fall and put her hands back in her lap. I must say I was almighty glad she did. Sitting there with her arms raised, her blouse was pulled tight across her chest. I was a lot more comfortable when she was sitting normal again.

"Have we escaped them, do you think?"

Well, there was no point in lying to her. "No, ma'am, Miss Janet. Not permanent, we haven't. I don't know for certain, of course, but I would bet that they can ride the long way around and find someplace they can get up here at us. It shouldn't be all that hard. They will likely find a way up and then start in a-looking for our hiding place."

"Will they find it? Our hiding place, I mean."

I grinned at her. "Ma'am, I figure that would be real *un*likely. You see, there won't be one to find. And I expect those boys will get some frustrated before they come to that conclusion."

"Whatever are you talking about, there won't be one? What are we going to do?"

I have to admit I was proud of what I had worked out. I was still grinning like a possum eating. "Simple, Miss Janet. We won't be here. You see, come sunup those ole boys down there will see that we aren't. Down there, that is. So they will take a look around. A careful look around. And given enough time, those ole boys will decide just exactly what we've gone and done." I chuckled a little.

"Now the next thing those smiling boys will do is just what I told you. They will come up here. Of course it will take hours. But then they know that we are afoot. And of course they will want to keep that advantage. Besides which they don't much strike me as the kind who'd walk when they can ride. So they'll ride right up here, just like I said. You've probably noticed already that those are some very confident boys and not in any big hurry. I, uh . . . I'm beginning to think they'd like to have you found without any . . . bullet holes, if you'll excuse the thought."

"You could be right," she put in. "There were several times during the past few days when they could have shot me. They didn't of course, but they did chase me further into this desert."

I didn't go and correct her, but if she thought this was a desert we'd been in then she'd never seen a real one. This was scrub but it was a far cry from being desert.

"Anyway," I went on, "it will take them a long time to get up here and an awful long time before they finally realize they aren't finding us because we aren't here. Or won't be by that time."

"Yes, but . . ."

"Yes'm. You see, as soon as we see those ole boys ride off to come find us, you and me are going to climb right back down the way we just come. And walk off to wherever we want. See?"

"Goodness, Mr. Williams, I think I do see." She giggled with pleasure, and I was almighty glad to be giving her something she could look forward to. Without that it would be an awful long night.

This time everything worked out just the way it was supposed to. Come morning we hid in some rocks near the edge of the drop-off. We made sure we couldn't be seen and then peered over the edge. Had a real good view of those good old boys figuring out where we had to have gone and riding off to look for a way up after us.

Well, we brushed ourselves off, climbed back down the way we'd come, and started walking, me with my saddle and bridle over one shoulder. Midmorning of the next day we hiked, blister-footed and aching, into a town called Friendly. We would have been happy to see it if it was called Hades and lay on the other side of a black and ugly river.

Now Friendly was what you might call a small town. There was a store, of course. The kind of place that handles everything from . . . well, the kind of place that handles just everything. There was a tumble-down shop built of logs, though all the other buildings were of sawn lumber. This shop was for a combination blacksmith-gunsmith-leatherworker. From the claims made on a whole flock of small, hand-lettered signs on his place, this fellow could fix anything that might be broke. He could weld and fit tires, shoe horses, build saddle trees, repair shotguns and revolvers, sharpen saws, replace spokes, repair windmill gears, make chaps, fix tools, and buy scrap metal. A useful man to have around, no doubt. If the owner of the store had been so thorough about advertising his wares, it would have taken the lumber from two forests just to make signboards to write it on.

There was the store, the shop, and three raggedy-looking houses. One of them had a pole corral and a lean-to shed behind it. The corral held a mule, a pair of heavy horses, and a fistful of saddle horses, so I took that place to be the closest Friendly could come to a livery stable. Not a building in town was painted.

The girl and me headed direct for the store. I dropped my kak on the front stoop and remembered in time to hold the door open for Miss Janet.

Inside, the store was a clutter of shelves and tables and benches, all of it piled with such things as hats and yard goods and potato ricers and oil lamps and hoes and spools of wire and canned foods. Here and there were piled sacks holding flour and salt and shot and heaven knows what more. Off in a far corner there were some kegs. Molasses and vinegar and nails and, more interesting, beer and whiskey. I was tempted but it would not have been polite.

The storekeeper was a man of forty-odd years. He was sitting in a rocking chair near a stove, cold and rusty under its coating of grease this time of year. He had an honest enough face although he wore no collar and his vest was unbuttoned. And he could have shaved more recent than he had. Not that I was in any position to criticize, you understand.

He got to his feet when we came in. He bobbed his head and smiled. "Glad to see you folks," he said. "What can I do for you today?" The way he said it, you'd have thought we were in the middle of a city and me and this girl dropped in three times a week at the very least.

I was ready to go through the whole song and dance about what we'd been through, but I no sooner had my mouth open to speak when the girl cut me off.

"Why, I am sure you can be of tremendous assistance, sir," she said. "Our name is Wolfe, sir. I am Miss Vera Jean Wolfe, traveling with my cousin Mr. Thomas Langston Wolfe." The way she lifted her chin when she said it, it was like she expected the storekeeper to know us by name even if he hadn't seen us before. It was obvious she had this all thought out in advance. Shoot, I like to believed it myself, the way she said it.

"We encountered some difficulty on the road, sir," she went on. "If you would be good enough to allow us use of your telephone we will proceed on our journey."

Now that girl had eyes. She could see as good as me there was no telephone exchange anywhere near this lonesome flat that held Friendly snug beneath the mountains. It could not have come as any surprise when the storekeeper told her so.

"I'm raht sorry 'bout that, Miss Wolfe, but there ain't no telephone nor telegraph either one this side of Apishapa City, and that's sixty mile from here."

"Oh dear," she said, just as shocked and surprised as a body could be. She turned to me. "What do you think, Thomas? Perhaps we should hire a rig to drive us to this Apishapa City."

I expect that had been the object of her little game to start with, but it did not work. The storekeeper nipped that off before the bud could blossom.

"Sorry, ma'am, but there ain't a rig to be had here. Closest thing to it would be Glen Maxfield's wagon, and it needs a wheel rebuilt before it could go anywhere."

"Oh dear," the girl said again. This time I think she meant it.

I barged in myself then, for I didn't want her coming up with an alternative plan before I had something to say. "Perhaps a saddle horse would be available, sir. I could attend to a portion of our needs myself while my cousin remains here to overcome the effects of her ordeal. In the meanwhile I can send a rig from the city to collect her." I thought it a nicely phrased speech, I did. The girl glared at me but not where the storekeeper could see. She'd started this game. Now she was stuck with it.

"Now that we can do, mister," the storekeeper said. "Glen has animals over to his place. He'd be glad to fix you up. The lady can stay with my missus until you get back with a rig." He seemed to be real happy to be of service. He took the girl by the arm and set her down in his rocking chair. "You set right here, Miss Wolfe. I'll fetch Mrs. Hogan for you an' get Mr. Wolfe on his way in no time."

Well, she was trapped. Like it or no, Miss Janet had to sit in that chair until "the missus" came to get her. So she sat.

The storekeeper and me went on about our business like we had forgot she was there. First we got a sack and filled it with things he thought I would need traveling since, late in the day as it was, I would have to stay the night on the road.

Of course I was playing the pilgrim to some extent, so I didn't mind when he loaded me down heavy with canned meats and canned beans and canned fruits. It wasn't that he was trying to sell more, either. He was afraid I might get lost and run out of food. I don't know how many times he described the road turns I should take so I could get to Apishapa City and not end up back in the mountains somewhere. It was thoughtful of him and I did appreciate it.

When we were done in the store he walked with me to the house with the big corral behind it. He called out a hallo when we got near.

The fellow who came to the open door was a lanky, bearded man with more than a portion of gray in his whiskers. He had a face like a hulled walnut and dark, lively eyes. He wore bib overalls and heavy shoes and looked more like a farmer than a horse trader.

The storekeeper introduced us, and we went around back. When I got a good look at the animals in that pen I was sure he was more farmer than horse trader.

"There they are, Mr. Wolfe," he said. "Good stock every one."

I looked at them and glanced at the storekeeper, but this man was his neighbor so I could not expect much of a comment from him.

There were five light horses in the enclosure and not a one of them looked fit to carry a kid herding milk cows. They were the roughest sort of scrub horses and if their story were known I expect they would turn out to be the culls some mustanger had caught and knew he couldn't sell to any kind of a horse buyer.

The wild horses of the mountains and deserts come from Spanish Barb stock, they say, and that is not blood to be ashamed of. But the years of uncontrolled breeding had allowed them to go

downhill. That was especially true since the mustang hunters had
been capturing horses and pulling out the best ones to break and
sell ever since the '60s or even earlier. They left the poorest stock
running loose to breed up more poor stock. That was one of the
reasons why Indians raiding off the plains used to pass by any
number of wild herds and risk their lives to steal good horses from
ranches and farms in more settled parts of the country.

Even though the mustangers were helping to breed themselves
right out of business, most of them were smart enough to shoot
the scrubs they caught in their traps. But it looked as if at least
one fellow had found someone gullible enough to buy his scrubs
too.

The light horses Glen Maxfield had in his corral still had their
forelocks clubbed into solid balls from the accumulation of burrs,
so I guessed they hadn't been handled very much. Most likely
they had been saddled and ridden down just once, then sold for
five or ten dollars as green-broke riding horses. It would be no fun
trying to top one of them the second time, and once you did you
would still have nothing for your money.

Maxfield didn't seem to know what he was paying to feed.
"They're all broke horses, Mr. Wolfe," he said. "You can have
your pick of them for twenty-five dollars." He pulled a stick of tobacco from a pocket and offered it around. When neither me nor
the storekeeper took any he sliced off a chew for himself and settled down to wait. After all, there wasn't anywhere else I could go
for a horse.

Well, I climbed between the rails of his fence and walked
around some, being careful not to get too close. They laid their
ears flat and kept sidling around so their rumps were pointed my
way ready for some quick kicking. It hadn't been any bright-eyed
and tenderhearted little girl that rode these animals before.

They were a fine, fair collection, they were. Sickle-hocked and
cap-jointed, ewe-necked and with as much rump as your average
hound dog. Finally I gave up and turned to Maxfield.

"There ain't a one of them will do, Mr. Maxfield. Not a one.
But I will give you that price for the mule yonder." I hooked a

thumb toward the gray mule standing patiently in the corner of the corral nearest Maxfield's little haystack.

I'd been watching that animal whilst I looked at the horses, and he was no pilgrim. He had his neck stretched low and looked half asleep but there was always one ear or the other turned my way. From the way the dapples in his gray coat had faded, I judged him to be twelve, give or take a couple years, which is still prime for a good-bred mule. He had a lot of leg to him, which would give him good speed at any gait. And there is nothing with a better ride nor that will go further on little feed than a good mule. I had decided to buy me that animal.

Maxfield pulled at his chin. "That mule'd pull a wagon, mister, but I don't know about you riding him. An' anyway I couldn't let him go for any twenty-five dollars. I got more than that in him."

"I could go a little higher," I said.

"I guess I'd take fifty for him."

"I guess I'd pay thirty-five."

Maxfield pulled at his chin again. "We could meet in the middle."

"We could if you throw in a breast collar an' breaching strap I can rig to my saddle."

"Done," Maxfield said. The way he and the storekeeper both smiled told me that Maxfield's bill at the store was not as big as I might have guessed.

I hiked back to the store alone to fetch my saddle and while I was there slipped some money from the belt under my shirt. I took a quick look in at the girl, too. So far the storekeeper hadn't taken time to call his wife, probably wanting to know how much Maxfield got in hand for the mule.

The girl was still waiting in the rocking chair. When she saw me looking in, she went to jump to her feet but I quick laid a finger to my lips, winked, and backed out of there.

It didn't take long to put the extra rigging on my saddle. Mules are built some different from horses, not so much rump and practically no withers, so unless you secure your saddle front and rear you can end up sliding all up and down the animal's back. Mostly they will not take to that as a good idea.

When I had everything cinched, buckled, and tied where it should be, I led the mule around a few steps to get him used to things, got a good grip on myself so to speak, and hoisted myself into the saddle. When he didn't blow up under me I smiled. He would do.

"What's his name?" I asked Maxfield, who was leaning against the fence beside the storekeeper, waiting to see if there would be any excitement.

Maxfield shrugged. "I just called him Gray."

I nodded. "Thank you kindly," I said. I put heels to my mule and the two of us went down the road.

CHAPTER 5

I rode out of Friendly feeling better than I had in some time. I had food in my sack, water in my canteen, and an animal under me again.

The mule wasn't my old horse, of course, but I was finding him easy to sit. He had been under saddle before. That was one of the first things I did when we were out of sight of Friendly. I tried that mule out a bit.

He took his gaits nice, with just the least amount of leg pressure. He turned with no more than a shift of weight. He even reined pretty and had a good stop on him. The darnedest thing about him, though, was one that set me to laughing right out loud, away out in the lonely with no one to hear but me and him.

You see, that gray mule had a smooth walk and a nice lope, but what got to me was his trot. That is a gait an animal can keep up practically night and day if it don't break the rider into little pieces. But this mule went as easy at the trot as a front porch glider. I couldn't figure it out at first. It felt all wrong. Then I paid attention down below and found that this old gray mule was pacing. He wasn't trotting at all but was swinging those long, bony legs of his back and forth just like a porch glider on rails.

I had heard of such a thing as a pacing mule but I'd never seen one before, much less ridden one. It was something you might expect to find bred into a fancy carriage horse or a harness racer. But a mule? For some reason that made me as tickled as a kid with a pup. I sat back in the saddle and grinned to myself.

I held him in that nice pace through most of the afternoon, going not toward Apishapa City but back the way we had come. I didn't follow direct on the foot trail we had made but held to one side of it so as not to blunder into the Trask boys unaware. I don't know where the girl thought I was going, but I figured I had me some business to take up with those boys.

It was not a pretty country I was passing through. The soil was dry, baked hard and brittle, and full of shale and ancient clays that gave it color but no life. It was lightly populated with sage and Russian thistle and occasional tufts of hardy bunch grasses.

From time to time I would see small groups of stock cows with their this-year calves prowling fitfully in search of forage. They were leggy, slab-sided creatures that showed much of the old longhorn range animal in their recent ancestry. I do not know where they might have watered, for here above the flats were no windmills to pump for them and the few watercourses were dry at this time of year.

Of wildlife I saw none save for a jackrabbit or coyote now and then. No mulie, sheep, or antelope was to be seen nor even any snakes in the heat of the day.

Not that I was spending my time looking at the scenery or watching the pretty animals go past. What I was doing was looking for the Trasks.

Unless those boys were a lot more thorough and a lot less imaginative than I was figuring, they should long since have found our tracks leading away from their trap and be following somewhere along that trail.

I had done what I could to slow them down in their trailing, and a person on foot does not leave much of a trail to start with. Which is why Indians often used to go on friendly horse-stealing raids afoot. That way they left no trail unless they were successful, and then it didn't matter. Of course I had not been able to be completely careful, not with the girl along, so I had no doubts that Ben and his brothers would be along sooner or later. That I had got so far on our back trail without running into them only meant that they were not very good at it and not that they could not do the job given enough time. And in a way I was counting on Ben's perseverance.

So I rode with caution through the afternoon until I was nigh to the bench face where we had last seen the Trask boys. They must have been some kind of persistent fellows, and I wager they knew the top of that table uncommon well by then.

When I came to the seep again—the only water I knew for certain hereabouts—there was still no sign of Benjamin and his brothers. I pulled the gray mule to a halt and watered him, then fed both him and myself while I waited for the boys to come along.

Unless there was another water hole on the other side of the table it was likely they would come back here to spend the night and get a start on tracking us in the morning. I didn't see how hardly anyone could be so single-minded as to think we would still be on the top of that rock table.

Still, I did not know the Trask boys overwell. They never did come to the seep that night and after considerable hours spent waiting in the darkness I led the gray mule off a ways and lay down for a sleep.

Come morning I stamped into my boots early and enjoyed some of the canned stuff from Mr. Hogan's shelves. I watered the mule from the seep and shivered a little while I did so. This was empty country, with no one around to tell the story should those boys come on me before I spotted them. Should that happen, I had little doubt of the outcome.

I made a point of staying close to the bench face where they would not be apt to spot me if they were still up above. I did not expect them to be there. But then again, I had expected to find them in camp at the seep the night before yet had found no sign of them save some days-old tracks. Since I hadn't been any too successful with those old boys so far, it seemed a poor time to be taking unnecessary chances.

Along about midmorning I was poking around the edge of the wall when I came unexpected to a deep cut running back into the face, well north of the water basin.

Standing there—as surprised as me—was young Tom Trask. What he was doing in there, and afoot at that, I could not understand.

I sat on my mule staring at Tom and he stood there staring back up at me for what seemed a terrible long time. Actually I suppose it wasn't long at all. Then Tom grinned. "Good to see you again, Mr. Williams," he said.

In a way I suppose it is a shame it wasn't Leo Trask I ran into there. If it had been Leo I don't doubt what would have happened. The two of us would have gone to shooting and maybe settled things on the spot, for good and all.

The way it happened, though, it was Tom, more like brother Benjamin than hot-blooded Leo, and before I made up my mind to build a fire inside my Remington he was grinning and talking. I have to say that it threw me off track somewhat. Which no doubt is just what Tom intended.

"It is a simply amazing coincidence," Tom said, casual as could be. "Here I am looking for someone to show me the way out of this desert, and you show up. Truly amazing, Mr. Williams."

"I take it you got yourself lost, Mr. Trask?"

"Indeed I did, sir. My brothers and I were looking for, uh, a trail. Footprints. As you can understand, I am sure. And I seem to have become separated from the others."

"Uh-huh," I said. It was about as intelligent a statement as I was capable of making at the moment. I mean there was something *special* about those Trask boys, Tom near as much as Benjamin. They could fix a stare on you with those clear, open eyes and just pour their furry little hearts out. Had they offered me some, I might of bought shares in a mining claim on the moon. Redeemable as soon as a railroad was built to there. I wouldn't even have asked to see the design work on the trestle.

By the time I realized how overinnocent Tom sounded, it was too late. Benjamin spoke up. From behind me.

"Thank you, Tom," he said. "You know I appreciate your thoughtfulness."

I turned around. Slow and with my hands nowhere near my gun. Ben and Leo were both there, both of them afoot too. I had no idea where they had left their pretty horses—which no cowhand would ever have done—but I had let them slip up behind me unheard while Tom was talking. I will admit to having a rather heavy feeling in my belly when I saw them.

Leo had a big-muzzled Colt leveled at the small of my back. He seemed to be enjoying that fact.

"You are just the person we have been wanting to see, Mr. Williams," Ben said. "Why don't you step down and talk with us?"

I shrugged my shoulders and swung down from the mule. There didn't seem to be much else that I could do.

Ben looked at Leo and nodded in my direction. I held both hands at ear level while Leo lifted my Remington and shoved it behind his belt. Leo was still looking pretty well satisfied with himself, especially when he slapped the barrel of his revolver across my cheek.

I won't say I was expecting that, but it was not a huge surprise either. I just kept looking into Leo's eyes until the force of it whipped my head around. It had about the same solid power of a six-month-old calf connecting with a hind foot. It brought tears to my eyes, and I could feel blood starting down my jaw. I left my hands where they were and looked Leo in the eye again.

"We wanted to ask you about our sister, Mr. Williams," Ben said. His voice was as smooth and easy as ever. I shifted my head enough to look at him, trying to ignore the fact that the initial numbness at my cheek was fast wearing away.

"I put her on a teamster's wagon hauling for Apishapa City," I told him. "That's the last I saw her or expect to see of her. I expect by now she'll be under the protection of whoever is town marshal there."

"Mmm, I don't much like the sound of that," Ben said.

"I can see how you wouldn't, but it happens to be the truth, Mr. Trask," I said. "Uh, do I need to point out that it also means that I'm no kind of threat to you now?"

Ben smiled. Leo cussed a little, the muzzle of his gun tickling me rather heavily in the ribs.

"If that is so, what would you be doing back here?" Ben asked in a pleasant tone of voice.

"Well." I rubbed at my jaw and wiped some of the blood away. "I did have some idea of asking you boys for the price of a good gelding. Or something to that effect. I suppose I could chalk it up to experience instead." I put it just as agreeable as I knew how. Which I guess was not quite agreeable enough.

"I don't think so, Mr. Williams. Judging from the effect of that little swipe Leo gave you, you are a well-controlled individual. If you were willing to let things pass for the benefit of the experience, I believe you would already have done so. And somehow I doubt that you would have handed our sister over to a teamster and gone merrily about your business. I simply cannot accept that, Mr. Williams."

I smiled at him. "If you can't, then I reckon you can't. Sure is a pity, though. I do hate to think of the alternatives."

"Mmm, yes. The alternatives. Leo is our specialist in those." His voice became more crisp. "Tom, lead the way on up. Leo, you keep an eye on our friend here. Do not allow him to become troublesome. I believe he could be if we gave him the opportunity."

Leo smirked at me. "I don't think so, Ben. Not mister meek and mild, here." At least I had Leo convinced of my inoffensiveness. He gave Ben a demonstration by punching me in the stomach, and I co-operated as well as I could. The next time he moved close to me I cringed away from him with my very best cringe. I think it made his whole day.

"What about the mule?" It was Tom speaking, the quiet one of the family. I reminded myself to watch out for him. He had handled himself right well while he was waiting for his brothers to show up.

Ben gave my mule a quick, annoyed glance. I got the impression Ben was not much for thinking in terms of livestock. "We can't take him up with us. Just leave him."

Tom's expression wasn't much for agreement, but he did not argue with his brother. He turned and walked deeper into the little cut where I'd found him. Leo gave me a helpful prod in the ribs with the barrel of his revolver, and I followed.

CHAPTER 6

The narrow cut formed a regular staircase to the top of the bench, maybe two miles north of where the girl and I had had so much trouble finding a way up at night. I had no trouble following Tom to the top and never once had to worry about poor footing. I was half tempted to take a fall, right on Leo, but with the other two boys there it likely would have been a foolish—and final —move.

Their big bay horses were on the top of the bench. Talk about strange sights. These good old boys had gone and made them a picket line to tie their horses to. They had strung a rope between two old and twisty-looking junipers and had all three horses tied to the rope by grass halters. It seemed downright silly to me, especially since I knew they had regular old hobbles in their gear. They'd used them the night I first met the Trasks.

Tied off to a rope that way, there was no way those bays could forage for themselves. And I didn't see any way the brothers could have hauled enough grain with them to keep their animals fit. It was a thing to remember, for it told me something about the Trasks and also might could mean that their horses wouldn't have much bottom right now if it came to a run.

Of course I was getting just a bit ahead of myself there. Brother Leo was still behind me with that big revolver he liked so well. And my old gelding had been proof enough that he could use it.

I followed Tom past the bay horses to a tight little camp the boys had set up. Their bedrolls were all rolled and tied. Their gear was secured to saddle hulls. Everything was neat and orderly. I never could of put together a camp that pretty, and I been living without a roof most of my life.

Tom paid me no mind. As soon as he reached the place he took some fresh wood off a little pile of the stuff and began stirring in the coals to start a new fire.

"That's far enough," Ben said, and Leo bumped me in the back with his revolver to emphasize his brother's order.

"Yes, sir," I said, trying to sound as timid as a whitetail doe. It seemed to please Leo. Ben glanced speculatively at his gun-happy brother and I decided I'd better go easy on that kind of thing. I didn't want Ben to get more ideas than he already had.

"Leo?"

"Yes, Ben?"

"Ask Mr. Williams about our sister."

"Yes, Ben."

Leo grimaced in what he apparently thought was an extra-tough expression. "Tell Ben about our dear sister, Williams," he threatened. His voice was halfway between a growl and a snarl. No doubt it was just the thing for intimidation purposes. Except I was worried about Ben and was more than a little tired of Leo.

"Sure," I said. "She's a nice enough gal, maybe a bit skinny, and about yea tall."

I held my right hand as if I was showing Leo how tall Miss Janet was. Stumpy the wise guy. But that put my extended fingers just below eye level with Leo and, what the hell, I thought. I whipped the ends of my fingers across his eyes backhand and again in the other direction. It must have stung him pretty good, for he jumped, and I planted the toe of my boot in his belly.

Then, quick, I stepped back, put my hands up in the air and did my best to dazzle Ben with a happy smile. Ben had his gun on me, of course, but by then Leo was losing his last meal all over himself.

I would say that that had to of been the highlight of *my* day. The rest of it was depressingly predictable.

Poor Leo was all for shooting me. When Ben refused to allow that, Leo tried to content himself with thumping on me. He thrashed and pounded for quite a while, and I must say that I got kinda tired of it. I was fresh enough at first to roll and slide, so Leo didn't do any real, down-deep damage. And after five or ten minutes of steady whacking, he hadn't the strength he'd started with. Still and all, it didn't do my appearance any good, and I was some tender at the end of it.

He got me good and bloody, and eventually I dropped off into what I hoped would pass as a faint. Darn near was one for real by then.

I was worried about would Leo take it up with his boots then, but I guess he was pretty tired. He gave me a couple halfhearted kicks and sat down beside the fire. He was huffing and blowing and greasy with sweat. I can't say that I had much sympathy for him over it.

I heard someone pouring coffee and Leo slurping it, then Tom said, "You forgot to ask him about Jan."

"Yeah," Leo said between puffs. "Guess I . . . did at . . . that."

"Later," Ben said. "But you surely are in terrible condition, Leo."

Leo muttered something vulgar. "That's more . . . exercise than I've had . . . in quite a while."

"Just think how bad you'd feel if he'd been fighting back," Tom said dryly.

Even without seeing it I could imagine how Leo would bristle at that. "Are you ready to go round next, Tommy?" His voice was sharp.

"Shut up," Ben said. "Both of you. We have better things to do than this."

"Name one," Tom said.

"Most importantly, we need to find Janet."

I heard a movement of some kind. "Go right ahead." It was Tom again.

"As soon as Williams comes to, we'll ask him."

"He could be out for hours," Leo said. He sounded so proud of the idea I thought I would take it as a suggestion. Especially when Ben said, "Well, as soon as he starts to stir you can get some coals ready."

I heard someone add wood to the fire.

Now I'll tell you, it is no easy trick to lay still for a whole, hot afternoon. But I had an excellent incentive. So I laid there dripping both sweat and blood and never moved, even when from time to time one of them would take a notion to prod at me.

"Do you think I killed him?" Leo asked after a long time.

"No. Not yet anyway," Ben said. "He's breathing all right. He might be dying, but he will come to before he does."

"What if he doesn't?" It was Tom's voice.

"Then obviously we must get along without his help." There was a short pause and Ben went on. "I think what we should do is take a look around, perhaps down toward that spring where he took Janet before."

"Why?"

"He would not have turned her over to a passing stranger. It seems logical to assume that Janet is waiting for him somewhere close by. It is getting on toward evening, and I imagine she should be growing restless by now. It should be a good time to look for movement."

"I don't know that I . . ." Ben cut Tom off before he could finish whatever he might have said.

"I didn't ask you," Ben snapped. "Leo, stay here. If that derelict cowboy comes to, drop a pan of coals in his lap or something to get his attention. Tom and I will walk down the rim a few miles to see if we can get along without asking him any more questions."

Leo grunted. With pleasure, I thought. I heard the other two hike off on foot. Apparently neither of them found anything wrong with the idea of walking when there were three perfectly good horses standing right at hand. Well, that was fine with me.

I laid there, still as I could manage, and picked over my arms and legs as best I could without moving. I tightened and relaxed the muscles in each limb, one at a time, and everything seemed to be working the way it should. I thought I had a pretty fair idea of what I could expect from Leo Trask.

Sure enough, his brothers hadn't been gone more than ten minutes or so before Leo got restless. He paced around by the fire and every time his feet stopped moving I thought I could feel his eyes drilling into my back. Then he'd pace and stomp some more. It wasn't long before I heard him shoveling something into a pan, and I had just too good an idea of what it was making all the clatter. Leo had him some coals and wasn't going to wait any longer. Brother Ben's idea had just been too good for him to resist.

I heard him walking toward me, and the skin on the back of my neck began trying to draw together. It was getting on toward evening and starting to cool off, but now I was sweating worse than I had during the heat of the day.

I could feel it as much as hear it when Leo's boots stopped just at the small of my back. I wanted to jump up and run so bad I nearly did it before I got control of myself, and I must have twitched because I heard Leo grunt. And all this time I could imagine a pan heaped full of red-glowing coals held over my bloodied ear and throat. I could practically feel the heat.

There wasn't much sense in trying to put off what I had to do now. It was the only chance I figured to have, so I had to take it. Reminding myself not to give it away by trying to collect myself into a better position first, I just turned everything loose and heaved against the ground.

I rolled backward against Leo's legs and at the same time yelled at the top of my voice.

I must have startled him pretty good, for I found I was too darn weak for the impact to have done much.

Anyway, Leo jumped in a sudden fright, and since I had rolled onto the toes of his boots he got off balance.

His arms flew up, and I had a brief view of a pot flying into the air and maybe a hatful of coals spewing out in all directions. Then Leo went down, stretched out flat on his back. He landed with a thud and I was already crawling and clawing up past his belt, pulling myself forward with my hands full of cloth and a head full of more rage and hurt and hate than I'd have thought possible. I could hear something growling like a cornered animal, and I suppose it must of been me making that noise.

I climbed up him, right past his gunbelt and holster without even giving them thought although by then Leo was kicking and twisting and trying to hammer clubbed fists into my face. I shoved what was left of my nose against the cloth of his shirt and kept crawling.

I've rode some crazy horses but never clung tighter than I did to Leo, and him bucking and rolling and trying to get away beneath me. Thank goodness he was so terrified by the unexpected suddenness of it that he never had time to think, for I was in no shape to stand him off in a fight.

I got hold of his shirt collar and pulled myself level with his face, and my blood and sweat made an ugly smear on his cheek. I think by then he was hollering, maybe for help or maybe just in fear, but I don't remember for sure. I could hear the dull sounds that were made as his fists thudded into my back and my ribs, but I could not feel the blows. Not then.

I do remember some of the white-hot desire to kill him then. And I don't fully understand it, but there was some impulse driving me. I was face to face with him, and he rolled his head to the side. When he did I clamped my teeth on his ear and tried to tear it away from his head. I could taste blood—my own or maybe his, I don't know.

At the same time I pulled my hands up to his throat and started to squeeze. I wanted more than anything else in this world to reduce the size of his neck so I could get one hand wrapped around it and hold it there as a protection against Leo and his panful of hot coals.

The next thing I remember is looking at Leo's face—dark, ugly red almost to the point of being purple—and knowing he was dead, that sometime during all this Leopold Trask had died. His lips were drawn back in a snarl that would never leave his face. I felt a revulsion as great as my hate had been, and I rolled off his body.

Rocks and small, spiny plants dug into my back, but I did not mind. My shirt was saturated with sweat and the drying of it felt cool and relaxing.

For a moment a deep weariness flooded through me and I was tempted close to healing sleep. Then I realized what that would mean and of a sudden I was fully awake, alert to every sound and every sight around. Ben and Tom would be back soon, and if they found me there would be no other chance for escape. They might have heard and already be racing back to the camp.

I got quickly to my feet, too anxious to feel any pain from the movement.

The bay horses were standing tied on their picket rope, nervous but not trying to pull away. I could not see Ben or Tom anywhere in the rock and scrub of the flat rim, and I noticed that the horses had their full attention on me. They had seen no movement nearby.

My first impulse was toward the bays, but then I remembered how little strength they should have. I did not want Ben and Tom following me, even on foot, with a quickly jaded horse under my saddle.

The mule was down below, though, and he had been well fed and well rested, starting fresh just the day before. It seemed much longer but was not.

I took my own revolver from Leo's body and, feeling somewhat more assured with it in place, began the hobble-footed walk back down off the bench. It was not comfortable to have to walk so far so soon but it seemed infinitely preferable to waiting for Ben and Tom Trask to return.

I picked my way down the incline, careful of every placement of my boots. Every footfall sent sheets of pain through my back and ribs, and I took no chances on falling through carelessness. The narrow path seemed far steeper going down than it had when we ascended, and I had unpleasant visions of how it would feel to slip and tumble down from rock to rock.

My attention was wholly on the path and so I did not notice until I reached the bottom that there was something dreadfully wrong there. The cut into the face of the bench was empty save for a small mound of manure. The mule was not there.

Forgetting the cost in pain, I raced to the opening and looked north and south along the sheer, barren face.

Whether he had been led or ridden away—perhaps by Tom—or if he had simply wandered away in search of graze and water, I did not know.

Whatever had happened, the simple truth remained. The transportation I had been counting on was not there. I was afoot.

CHAPTER 7

I felt dazed and for a moment I was close to panic. I pulled the Remington and with it in hand backed into the cut, trying to look in all directions at once.

When I realized what I was doing I forced myself to put the gun away and to sit down on a nearby boulder. Those simple physical actions seemed to help. At least they were reasoned acts of a sort and not blind reaction.

There were still several choices open to me despite the loss of the mule. As far as I knew, Ben and Tom still assumed that Leo had things under control at the camp. They might return at any minute or they might not come in for hours, hoping to see firelight if they waited for full darkness.

The bay horses were still on their picket line. I might have time to take them. All three of them. Or I could take the offensive. Hide near the Trasks' camp and hope to get lead into Ben and Tom before they knew they were in danger. I could place Leo's body on the ground where I had been lying. They might not notice the substitution if it were dark when they returned.

The more I thought about it the better that idea sounded. It might be murder committed from ambush from their point of view, but it seemed an effective line of defense from mine.

I gave no real consideration to the idea of trying to get away from them on foot. Not in the condition I was in.

Already my muscles were starting to stiffen, and the pain of each movement was bone deep. Even breathing, anything deeper than short, shallow breaths, sent fiery lances of pain through my chest and ribs. And I had no intention of stopping that activity. Not as long as I had anything to say about it.

I looked at my hands in the fading light and was satisfied. They were sticky with blood but were not themselves damaged. I had had little enough opportunity to hit Leo, and his blows and kicks had been concentrated on my face and torso. Those aches and the sharp, coppery taste in my mouth from cuts inside the cheeks would not affect my ability to use a gun. And I hoped that the tremors of fatigue would not appear when I had need of a steady hand. I flipped open the loading gate of the Remington and put a sixth squat cartridge into its cylinder. An empty chamber was safer for carrying, but now I might need the firepower more than that margin of safety.

Resigned to what I had to do, I shoved myself upright and began the long climb back onto the bench.

By the time I regained the top I knew that at the very least Leo had broken several of my ribs. I felt lightheaded and weak and had too little control over my knees. Trying to keep my own legs under control seemed as futile as trying to push a rope. From time to time they would buckle without warning, and twice I sprawled full length onto sharp rocks and sun-baked earth. It did not make me feel any better.

By then, too, it was dark and I was having trouble seeing where to place my feet so I would not either fall or make any more noise than was absolutely necessary. Oh, that was a bully experience, it was.

When I got close to the camp I got down on hands and knees to creep the rest of the way in. I was better concealed that way, not so likely to show up against the early night sky if anyone was watching. And it kept me from announcing my presence by falling flat on my face.

It was just as well that I did sneak in quiet like that. There were two dark figures beside the black lump where I'd left Leo's body. I was close enough to hear some of what they said.

". . . probably try for the horses."

"Maybe."

". . . hope so. You . . ."

"He is bound to . . ."

"It makes no difference."

". . . if Leo was . . ."

"I don't care about that. Just make sure you do what you have to do."

". . . will, Ben."

"See that you do."

At least I knew what I was up against. It was small consolation at best.

I suppose I could have started shooting right there and then, but I wasn't even tempted. I was in no shape for a foot race if I should miss in the darkness. Instead I crept away, still on hands and knees and not daring to think of how miserably symbolic that might have been. Those rannies sure seemed to have the upper hand. But then again, the odds were shorter than they had been, and there was a gun ready to my hand.

For the second time that evening I made my way down off that bench. The second time, in darkness, was certainly no easier than the first had been.

When I hit what passed for level ground again I didn't waste any time resting. I went south along the face. My progress was slow—I had no choice about that—but I kept at it steady and after a while I made it to the water seep where I'd stopped before. It was still the only water I knew of close by, and I needed it bad.

When I reached the seep I got down beside it and ducked my head as far under as the rock bottom would allow, then I tried my best to drink it dry.

The water burned something awful when it hit the cuts and scrapes on my face, and there were more of them than I'd realized. But it was worth it. I splashed some on my neck and chest and felt a little better anyway. When I absolutely couldn't hold any more water I rolled over onto my back and lay there hoping to come up with some marvelous plan for getting out of this mess.

It is just as well that I did not really expect to find one. No amount of wishing or dreaming was going to change what was into what might have been. I shook off a case of the what-ifs and got down to some serious thinking.

I was in no condition to go very far on foot. Not very fast, anyway. I didn't know where to find more water. And I had no way to carry any of this water with me. My canteen was on the mule, wherever that was. Given daylight and enough time, I could have tracked him, but it was certain the Trasks would not be that generous. Those boys were persistent if they were anything at all.

Given a horse or the mule, I could make it to water somewhere else. To known water at Friendly or away back on the flat at a windmill trough or somewhere around here if I poked into enough likely places. But the Trasks had the only horses handy.

Given a little time and a little luck, I could shoot a cow or a desert sheep or an antelope or something and make a water sack from some tied-off guts or a bladder. But the Trask boys would just love to have me tell them where to find me by making big noises.

I was tied by the need for water, and it surely seemed that I was tied to this particular seep. There had to be water somewhere close to their camp. But where? And what good would it do me if I did know?

Then I got to thinking on that. What good *would* it do if I knew where they were getting their water?

All right, I thought. They know about this seep. They know I've used it at least once before. This is where they came looking for Miss Janet earlier this evening. So they will expect me to use this water again. They will be watching it, which is as good a reason as any for using another water hole if I can find one.

So how do I find another? Let them show me where it is. They'll expect me to get as far away from them as I can. That's why they are guarding their horses so close. Right? Seems so. All right then, lay up somewhere close to their camp and watch them when they water their horses in the morning.

Yes, but to do that I have to go all that way back. And I hurt. So all right. Be lazy. Maybe be dead. Then you won't feel a thing, idiot.

Score one for going back. But I'll leave tracks if I do. No way to avoid it.

Yes, but those boys have demonstrated pretty well that they couldn't trail a cow in fresh snow. Otherwise they wouldn't still be messing around out here while Miss Janet is miles away visiting with a shopkeeper's wife.

And otherwise you wouldn't be out here beat to a pulp and on the run. Who's on the run? And I thought there wouldn't be any more of the what-ifs. I apologize.

Idiot.

Idiot, yourself. You talk about it, but I notice you're laying here beside a water hole instead of tramping all that way back to the Trasks' camp.

You're right.

I rolled over and sucked up more water until I positively could hold no more, forced myself to drink two more swallows, and got to my feet with a groan.

If anything I was aching worse than when I laid down, but I felt stronger. Not much, but maybe enough. I turned and started walking north.

There was no higher ground I could watch from, so the best I could do was to belly in fairly close and hide myself as well as I could in a clutch of thorns and leaves in the scrub. It seemed entirely illogical to be flinching away from a few little thorns—what harm could they do that wasn't already done?—but I did it anyway. It took quite a while to get reasonably comfortable.

The place I had chosen was not a good one, but nothing better seemed to be available. If one of the Trasks should come anywhere near in daylight we would have to shoot it out on the spot, and I had little desire to face the two of them. Especially since they had carbines slung on their saddles and I had only my revolver. I should have had sense enough to take Leo's when I had the chance, but it was too late now.

Because I did not want to be seen I had wormed my way around to the west of the camp, away from the path down the bench face and away from the direction they would likely take if they wanted to watch the seep from above. It was strictly a toss-up about which way they would head toward water. I only hoped it would not be toward me.

I hadn't long to wait until morning, it had taken so long to get back and into position without them or the horses seeing me. I did not know if Ben or Tom could correctly guess about the flick of a horse's ears and I did not want to take a chance on it. A horse can tell a reasonably observant person quite a bit about what is going on around him, and this was no time to be underestimating the Trask boys' experience.

I passed the time waiting by avoiding going to sleep—no mean trick, that—and by listening to my belly rumble. I might have fairly simple tastes but I like to satisfy them regular, and it had been a good, hard day since I'd had anything to eat.

About daybreak Ben took my mind off food by raising up out of the brush not more than forty feet away from where I was hid myself. Thank goodness my stomach hadn't growled any louder. It's a wonder he hadn't heard it as it was. And me with no idea old Benjamin was so close. He must have been asleep when I crawled in, was all I could figure. I can move pretty quiet when I want to, but that was more of a test than I would have wanted to try.

Ben stretched and stamped and forced back a yawn. He bent and picked up his carbine, a pretty Sharps-Borchardt it was and about the best that money could buy, and called to Tom. "You can come in now." He took a quick look around the horizon, and his eyes swept right over me. And right on past.

It is a funny thing about that. Or maybe that is a poor choice of words, for a lot of men have died because they did not know it and so there can be little humor in it. Apaches know it, though. The thing is, if a man is watching for someone who might be attacking him—or for a deer or other game for that matter—he tends to focus out toward the far end of his visual range. Out toward the horizon. Along the edge of a patch of woods. At the top of the next hill. Get somewhere inside that circle of attention and you won't be seen as long as you are motionless. Any sort of movement will draw the eye but not a still shape, not even one clothed in relatively bright colors.

That is why an Apache can crawl up to a man in broad daylight in places where you wouldn't think a mouse could be hid. It's the same with a deer. Wait until the head is down to feed and you can move on. When the head comes up, stop. When it is a man, they move when he is looking away; stop when his eyes swing back. It works. I know. For from where Ben was standing I was in plain sight of him, and he never knew it. He turned and walked back to their camp.

Tom joined him there and they talked briefly. I was too far away then to hear. Ben stooped to stir up a fire and get a breakfast started. Tom turned toward the horses. It was what I had come all that long, miserable way from the seep for.

The younger of the brothers, or so I figured Tom to be anyway, untied the lead ropes from the picket line and led the bay horses away to the north. Seeing that much should be all I would need, for I had the direction now and could read their tracks to the water as soon as Ben and Tom went off to search for me or Miss Janet.

Those bay horses did not look as slick now as they had a couple days before. They had had some hard use and must have been pulled off their grain ration for several days. Worse, the Trasks had not allowed them free grazing when they were not under saddle. The bays were being treated like cavalry mounts, except the Army always carries full forage and grain rations with them.

When I first saw them those bays had still been as sleek as a wet pup. Now the bloom was going off their hair, starting to go dull, and while they were yet far from being gaunted you could see rib lines just under the skin on their sides. It seemed a shame.

I lay there waiting for Tom to come back and watched Ben fussing around in their camp. Part of what he was doing was obscured by the brush between us, but he seemed to be spending his time at the fire. I was just as glad that the wind wasn't carrying the smell of food to me. That would have been hard to take.

After half an hour or so Tom came back—without the horses—and sat down to his breakfast. Well, I guessed that the Trasks could see a rib as easy as me, and it took no talent to know that a horse has to eat. The thing that worried me was that they might split up and each one guard a different water hole, one of them protecting the horses at the same time. That could be troublesome.

When they finished eating Ben kicked the fire apart while Tom stowed everything into the proper bags or bundles.

They seemed ready to leave when Tom said something to Ben

and he turned back toward their gear. I could see him bent over something and when he straightened he had a second carbine in his hand. It was another Sharps-Borchardt. Tom was carrying a repeater that from the shape of the lever I took be a Kennedy.

Ben said something to Tom and appeared to be offering him the more accurate single shot Sharps. Tom shook his head. His brother shrugged, looked at the carbine—it must have been Leo's —and started smashing it on the ground.

He held it by the barrel and flailed at the ground until the butt-stock had broken off and the finger lever was twisted all out of shape. He tossed it aside. I had no doubt that it was as useless a lump of metal now as it had been before it was machined. Good for a doorstop or a paperweight. No more.

When they walked away, though, I started to get excited. *Both* of them were heading south. Toward the seep I had left those hours before. With them out of the way . . .

I was so wound up about the possibilities before me that I was almost able to forget all the bruises and cuts and other hurts. I made myself wait for a solid fifteen minutes and then slipped forward, toward their camp.

My ribs burned until I was reluctant to breathe, but the effort was definitely worth it. I slid into their camp, crawling most of the way snake-like. I was taking no chances now.

Ben had smashed the carbine and left it useless, but there was something there that was much more important to me right then. They'd left their food unprotected.

I went straight to the sack where they kept their eatables and with my knife hacked open a can of peaches. I finished off the soft, golden fruit and drank away every bit of heavy, sweet syrup and felt some better. It was the first food I'd had in too long. Then I did the same for a can of tomatoes.

That was all the canned food they'd had left, but it was enough. I couldn't have held more. They also had a mostly depleted sack of flour, which I left be, and the rind end of a slab of smoked bacon. That I wrapped in a cloth and shoved inside my shirt. There was no question of starting a fire in the near future but it might come in handy, so I took it.

Then, feeling a whole lot better, I looked around as careful as I could. There was no sign of the Trasks. Keeping as low as possible, I began following the trail left by Tom and the bay horses. At the end of those tracks should be water and a trio of horses to carry me out of range of the Trask boys. For the moment.

CHAPTER 8

The bay horses were hobbled, but there was no need for them to be. They were not about to leave that patch of grass, dry and sparse as it was, without someone forced them away from it. They were going after it like they hadn't eaten in days, and maybe they hadn't.

There were some upthrust fingers of rock at the rim of the bench, and it was with considerable relief that I sank into a puddle of shade at the base of one. The heat of the sun was almost enough to match the fire in my ribs, but that was all right. I didn't mind in the least. Things were going almighty well, everything considered. The Trask boys were three, maybe four miles away and right in front of me not seventy-five yards off were three horses. It was more than I could have hoped for just a few hours earlier.

I still hadn't seen the water hole I was expecting to find here, but that was all right. I could get along without that for the moment. With a good horse under me I had no worries about water. Nor about getting to a place where I could rest up and go on the mend. I needed that bad, but already I was not feeling so desperate for it. I was willing to take my time and look things over before I moved out into the open to collect the horses.

The rock I was propped up against was right at the edge of a sheer drop off the bench. The rim here was ragged, with several of these fingers jutting above the normally flat edge and with a scattering of loose rock and small boulders on the surface. It hurt to twist my shoulders but by craning my neck around to the right I could see past the rim to the ground maybe a hundred feet below. The rock here seemed particularly rotten, for the ground below was littered with fallen slabs of basalt and a loose fan of broken scree.

It was a barren and unattractive place and not where I would have expected to find water. I suppose that should have told me something, but it did not.

On the flat away from the rim were some tufts of dusty gray-green bunch grasses and some low gray brush. The ground here was a little gray as well. All in all a fairly depressing place in appearance. Not that I was so affected by it at the moment.

Except for the bays there was no movement. No birds or animals were evident, and at this time of day there was not even a puff of wind to stir the taller stems of grass. The sky was bright and held only a single cotton ball of cloud. It hung as motionless as if it were one painted on canvas and hung on a parlor wall. The horses shifted their heads from tuft to tuft and occasionally shuffled their feet to bring more stems in reach of their mobile lips. Beyond that there was nothing.

I was beginning to feel some rested and started thinking about moving out toward the horses. It had been a fair amount of time now and nothing had offered any sign of motion.

Using the tall finger of rock for support, I pulled myself to my feet. It started all the aches to hurting again after the rest and relative comfort of sitting still for a while.

I felt a sharp spasm of pain in my chest and turned, thinking to lean against the rock a moment before I walked out to the horses.

There was a sudden flick of motion at the edge of my vision and if I'd had time I would of cussed out loud.

I felt something smash into my body with all the brutal force of a blacksmith's hammer. I was flung against the rock and tumbled away from it.

For one awful instant, distorted in time until it seemed a long while, I hung suspended at the edge of the rim, my feet still in contact with the ground and the upper part of my body out over clear air and nothing more.

Then I was tumbling free. Gray rock flashed past my eyes and I tried to reach for a handhold. Then something rushed up and hit me hard in the stomach.

I was half conscious, dizzy and sick, and only barely alive, and I knew it. But I *was* alive. At that moment I did not really care.

Voices floated around me and I was dimly aware that they came from above. I listened to the words without interest in their meaning.

"How did he get there without either one of us seeing him come?"

"I don't know, but I think it startled me as much as it did you."

"He just popped up out of the rock from nowhere."

"It makes no difference now. We don't have to worry about him any more. He was only a mild annoyance at worst."

"Except for Leo."

"Yes. Except for Leo, damn him."

"What do we do now?"

"We look for Janet, of course. She does not seem to be around here, so the next logical step would be to look in Apishapa City."

"That's where he said she had gone."

"True, but I had not suspected he might be telling the truth. As it is . . ."

"I'll get the horses and get ready to go, then."

"Right. You do that."

I heard gravel crunching under a boot. Moments later there was another sound. A faint, metallic *clack*. It was just as well the sound was too faint for me to identify it.

There was a booming roar above and again something smashed into me. I could feel the blow against my back. Interestingly enough it was my stomach that hurt. From where it was pushed against the rock beneath me.

After that I felt nothing. I never heard Ben walk away.

The next thing I remember is a deep-seated leaden feeling in the pit of my stomach. I more or less remembered that I'd been shot, but it was my stomach that was bothering me.

I came awake slow, drifting in and out of a sort of sleepy daze, annoyed by the stomach-ache but otherwise not too much concerned about things. I must have hung in that state for quite a while because by the time I really knew what was going on around me I was in full shade, and the rock under my hands was cool to the touch.

I flopped my head over to the side and lay for a moment enjoying the feeling of cold stone against my cheek. I seemed to have a bit of a fever.

Then I remembered why that might be, and I began to take stock of what all I could feel. I moved my arms by just the smallest amount and my whole left side felt as if it had been bathed in a tub of molten iron. I think I cried out loud.

Putting as much of the work as I could on my right arm, I levered myself up and half turned to a sitting position. I was wedged against a short, jutting spear of rock, slap against the bench face. It was an area too small to call a ledge. Just a chance projection out from the face that had arrested my fall.

The ground was maybe eighty feet below and behind where I was now half sitting, half laying. Immediately before me was solid gray rock. I raised my eyes and found that the rim I had fallen from was a good twenty feet away. It was not a comforting thought.

The upthrust angle of my perch gave support behind me to just above the small of my back. I leaned against that and used my right hand to feel of my left side. My shirt there was caked hard and crinkly with dried blood, and I wondered idly how long it would have taken to dry so.

Beneath the stiff cloth I could feel at least two wounds. One was toward the back and well over to the side. It was a small puncture, and I figured it to be the first shot I'd taken. The other was by far the worse of the two. It was lower and much larger, with torn, ragged edges of flesh. It had to be the exit wound from where Ben had shot me in the back after I'd fell. That meant there would be another opening or two around where I couldn't reach them. Not that it seemed to make much difference now.

I had no illusions about what was to come. Ben thought he had killed me.

He probably had.

I would probably make things a whole lot easier for myself in the long run if I just kicked away from the projection that was holding me and plunged the rest of the way down to the broken rocks below.

The only people anywhere around that I might call to for help were the Brothers Trask. And it seemed unreasonable to think that they would have a sudden change of heart if they learned I was still, more or less, alive.

For that matter, they might no longer be in hearing of a gunshot signal either. It came back to me that they'd been pulling out for Apishapa City after they disposed of old Stumpy. And they sure seemed to have done that.

For no good reason I tucked that scrap of knowledge away in a corner of my mind just like I might have use of it at some time in the future.

It was depressing to know that I wouldn't have future need of that fact. I peered over my projection and looked at the ground far below.

I suppose I should say how I thought about going ahead and jumping, but the plain truth is that I had no such notion. It just wasn't in me to give in to the Trasks that easy. I *knew* I was going out, but I'd darn well be kicking and clawing the whole way. What I was looking for on that rock face was a way down the darn thing.

Couldn't find one, though. Off to each side of where I was, the rock was jagged and gouged from where it had been crumbling. Directly below me it was smooth and sheer. No doubt it was some quirk of hardness in the rock structure that made it so. The same harder rock composition that put my little projection there also made the face beneath it so awful smooth. But I guessed I couldn't have it both ways at once. If it hadn't been like that I'd already be dead from a hundred-foot fall. Instead I had a good chance to die from thirst or loss of blood or an eighty-foot fall. I started to shrug but it hurt too bad and I gave it up.

I had to start doing something reasonably constructive if only to keep from thinking about my troubles, so I began fumbling at my belt buckle.

My fingers brushed a lump under my shirt, and I remembered the chunk of bacon I'd stolen from the Trask camp. I fished it out of my shirt and found that it was none too pretty. It was slick with grease and blood and sweat, and raw bacon has never been of much appeal to me. Still, it was food, all the food I had, and if anything could help me it would be to get some strength back. I was fresh out of that at the moment.

I laid the bacon down so I could wipe it off, and I think I managed to get more grit on it than I got grime off it, but I felt better about it anyway. I took a good hold on it and commenced gnawing on the least filthy end.

The way that raw bacon went down it should have choked a buzzard, it tasted so bad, but I kept at it. It was like chewing gum rubber but I managed to tear off and swallow some without losing it. I can't say that I felt any better for doing it.

When I'd done my duty with the bacon I laid it aside, what was left of it, and went back to my belt buckle.

I tried to take off my belt the usual way, but my left hand was not co-operating so I had to clumsy it open one-handed. I slipped the belt from its loops finally and laid it up too. Then I set in one-handed to attacking the knot of my bandanna.

When I eventually got that loose I folded it into a reasonable neat wad and slipped it under my shirt to cover the ragged exit wound of that last bullet. Of the holes I could reach I figured that was the one most likely to open and give me trouble.

It was quite a trick then trying to get my belt tightened in place over my makeshift bandage. I don't doubt I would have made a purely laughable sight had there been anyone around to watch.

It was enough of a trick just getting the belt around back of me to where I could reach it on both ends. Working with one hand and trying not to twist my shoulders, it was real interesting.

I tried passing the belt down over my shoulders, but it wasn't long enough for that. Every time I let go of one end, the free end would fall off out of place to where I couldn't reach it again.

I tried throwing it around from the right to wrap around behind and wind up on my left side. That would have worked if I could have grabbed it with my left hand once it got around there, but of course I couldn't. About all I was able to do that way was to twice flap the leather against one of the wounds on my back that I hadn't been able to investigate yet. I gave up on that.

What finally worked was to hook the belt under my left arm and pull it up with the buckle wedged crossways at the front of my armpit and the leather tailing out to the rear. Then I held the free end and let the belt fall behind me until I had it all the way around.

Next I had the problem of trying to trap both ends in one hand and get the end threaded into the buckle, with the belt over the bandage. Oh, it was bully sport, it was. I'm sure it would have had me in stitches if I'd been a spectator.

Well, I got it done finally and was ready for the hard part. I took as deep a breath as I dared and got my nerve up for what was to come. Then, hard, I hauled that belt in tight. I guess I hollered some before I passed out.

I can't say that I felt any better when I came to again. It was getting on toward dark, and I was almighty thirsty. I wasn't in danger yet from lack of water. Not quite. But it had been the night before since I'd had anything to drink, and I had lost considerable blood since. I knew I couldn't count on having much strength left in reserve. When I started to go down I would go fast.

To hold it off as long as I could, I ate some more bacon, quite a bit this time. The salt on the bacon and the knowledge that I didn't have any water did nothing to ease my desire for it, but there was not a darn thing I could do about it. I tried without a whole lot of success to put it out of my mind.

Everything I'd done so far, I realized then, was just a way of putting off my real problem. If I was going to get down off that bench face, how the devil was I going to do it?

There was no question that an eighty-foot drop would kill me, so the only choice seemed to be up. I took a look upward and was not much encouraged. In fact I was purely disheartened.

I could see four, maybe five good handholds on the face above me. Those and maybe three more that would not be good at all but might have been better than nothing.

The problem was that the one closest to me was perhaps six

feet above where I was now lying and about eight feet out to the right. It would take good balance and a perfectly timed leap to reach it. Moreover it would require a sure grip to hold on once I reached it. And there was no way I could raise my left arm, much less get a good grip with my left hand.

Assuming I could make that jump, it was another four feet up and a foot left to the next higher hold. I would be hanging free, unable to get any drive from my legs. To make it up there, I would have to chance everything on a dead left arm.

From there—if I made it that far—I might use the first place for a foothold and the second as a handhold, but I'd have to go to the left again another five feet and up three to reach a decent hold. If I slipped on that one I would probably fall back to where I'd started from, but I would be stretched out to land on my left side, right on the bullet wounds. It did not look promising.

Above that were enough holds that I just might could make it within four feet of the top.

But without good toe purchase, depending solely on the power of one arm . . . I just didn't know. It seemed like a more painful way to jump over the edge.

I studied that face closer than I've looked at anything, ever, and could find no other path, no other idea. It seemed sure death.

The only question, though, was when to try it. I would *not* lay still and wait to die. I would *not* end it of my own free will. I had to do something, even if I failed.

So when to go? I lay and looked and pondered until it began to get dark, and I realized I had been putting it off. The simple truth is that I was scared. I did not believe I had any chance of getting up that face, but I could think of nothing else to do.

I admitted that to myself and felt some better when I did. It was getting too dark to see the handholds now, but I wasn't using that excuse. Instead I was deliberately putting off what I expected to be my last act.

As soon as I decided that, I felt at least a little better. I still had some control over things.

I put my head down, smelling dust and bacon grease and myself, and went to sleep, wedged there on that cold rock spear.

CHAPTER 9

I knew I was mostly asleep but I didn't mind. I didn't really want to wake up. I was too comfortable to want to lose what I had in exchange for the real world. Here I was laying on a bed so soft I felt like I was floating. My arms and legs had to be somewhere, but I could not feel them. I had no idea where they were except for knowing they had to be somewhere close by.

It was a delightful feeling. Much like swimming when you quit thrashing through the water and go limp and trust the water to hold you up. It was that same kind of light, floaty feeling. But as I got more and more awake the bobbing, floating sensation came closer to being waves of nausea, and when I tried to smile to myself it pulled the cuts at the corners of my mouth and I knew I'd have to wake up soon.

Besides, there was some sound—a scratching and tearing and dull, wet, thumping sound—that kept shoving itself in among my other, pleasant thoughts. After a little while I realized that those sounds were for real and not something I was putting into my own half-dream thoughts. Wondering what the sounds were brought me the rest of the way back to wakefulness. I was not grateful for the change.

I tried to open my eyes and found they were glued shut. It seemed too much trouble just then to hunt up my hands and put them to the task so I screwed my face up in a series of contortions trying to raise an eyelid. That got the cuts on my face to moving, and they stung so bad tears came to my eyes. It was enough to dissolve some of the pus or ooze that was there, and my left eye came open. The lid bounced up and down a few times and tried to tack itself shut again, but by dropping my jaw and raising an eyebrow I found I could make it stay open. Progress. A triumphant feat to commence the day. I was immeasurably pleased with myself.

I was tempted to reward myself by going back to sleep, or to whatever distant state I had been in, but I heard the sounds again and this time sensed motion to accompany the noises.

The movement was immediately before my one open eye, but at first I could not focus on it. An image was there but made no sense. Then it did. I had been trying to see something at a distance. This was within inches. As soon as I realized the problem I could see what it was.

It was a bird. A pinyon jay. It stood within inches of my nose, closer than I had ever seen a living bird of any sort. It was a chunky little thing, dark blue on the wings and back. The belly fluff was a slightly lighter blue and toward the throat it faded almost white. Its legs were scaled black armor that flexed ever so slightly when it moved. The beak was long and cruelly pointed, dull black for most of its length but polished with an oily gloss toward the tip. A quick black eye without capacity for any compassionate or even interested contact from one species to another was fixed on mine. It was not fearsome. Merely indifferent. Totally indifferent.

When I failed to offer the threat of motion it went back to its feeding and I understood the partial gloss on its beak. The oil was grease from my bacon rind. The small head with its rounded cap of deep blue feathers bobbed, and the sharp little beak plunged into the fat of the bacon with a miniature thump. Had I not been so close I could never have heard.

The jay held the rind down with one foot and pulled back with more power than I would have supposed. The beak scissored at the tough fat, and the head shook with vibrating quickness like a terrier killing a rat. It was rewarded with a tiny scrap of bacon. It pointed its head skyward and let the white morsel tumble down the length of the beak to its waiting mouth. Without pause it attacked the bacon again. From the tattered condition of the rind, the bird had been at this for some minutes.

It was interesting to watch. It was also my bacon the jay was enjoying, the only food I possessed. The jay could slip from the rock into winged flight on free air as a matter of course. I could not. That bacon might be my last link with survival.

Of course that was the optimistic point of view. Considering the sheer face above me it might be overly optimistic. Nevertheless I was not willing to abandon that link. If I didn't make it, the jay was welcome to come back and claim the bacon. And me too. Until then the bacon was mine.

I tried to shout at the jay to scare it away. A dry, rasping croak was all that came from my throat, but it was enough.

Blue wings fluttered in alarm, so close I could feel the air they disturbed. One black foot was still hooked around the chewed-up rind, and for a moment I thought the bird would lift both itself and the food.

Without thinking I tried to grab the bacon with my left hand. I got little movement from the arm but lots of pain. I tried again with my right. By then the jay had pulled the bacon beyond my reach.

The bird shrieked its anger and fluttered its wings all the harder, but the rind was too heavy. The jay released its hold on the contested eatable and flapped indignantly away. By then it was to late. The bacon had been pulled past the level edge of my projection.

Perhaps sped along by its own grease, the bacon rind went skittering and sliding downward along the bench face beneath me. I leaned forward and watched it go. Its passage left intermittent oily patches behind in a neat, upward pattern. The bacon, my bacon, ended up in a drift of grayish-yellow sand directly below and a half-dozen feet out from my perch. I could see it. There was no way I could retrieve it.

With a groan of combined disgust and pain I lay back against the solid rock of my projection. That small amount of movement had hurt. Worse than I would have expected, and I expected considerable. I was not in very good shape.

I lay still for a few minutes trying to pull some strength together from somewhere. But there was no point in trying to fool myself.

I looked up the face to the first handhold I would have to reach. Six feet up and an ugly eight-foot leap out to the right. *If* I could stand up it would be just over head height. An easy reach. But eight feet out to the side, with one arm hanging useless, a bunch of wounds eager to start bleeding again. And that only the beginning of the climb.

I looked at my right hand and made a fist. I was weak. My whole arm trembled from that small exertion. Loss of blood, shock, lack of water, lack of food. They were taking a rapid toll.

I knew what would happen. If I could manage, somehow, to reach that first handhold it would also be the last. I hadn't the strength to propel myself high enough or over far enough one-armed to reach the second hold. I would fall to the jagged rock scree at the foot of the bench. I stared down at the rocks where I knew I would fall.

I lay back and my thoughts were bitter ones. I could see my own body tumbling down from that handhold. Falling free to be crushed on the sharp rocks.

Falling. I could see it plain in my imagination.

But there was something wrong with the thought.

Something other than the obvious fact that I did not want to do it.

I looked at the handhold again and my eyes moved directly down the face. The rocks were there. Waiting to catch me in a final embrace. They lay pointed and hard edged at the back of a tiny cove, immediately below the handhold. Exactly where I must surely fall.

There was something wrong about that. I could see myself falling. Yet there was another image in my mind. A remembered image, not an imagined one.

The *bacon*.

That bacon hadn't fallen and bounced. It slithered and slid and twisted from its own weight, but it never once dropped free. And it landed in a drift of sand.

Excited for the first moment since that bullet had ripped into me, I craned my neck to again peer over the side of my perch.

Sure enough, there was a slope, steep but definitely angled. At the bottom of it was my piece of bacon.

The only way I could figure it was that this section of harder rock where I was laying projected downward like that or else by sticking out when wind and water wore everything else away from it, it had protected the softer rock below. Whatever the reason, I was at the top of a long, steep slope on the face of the bench.

I shoved with my legs until I could see better below the projection and from there I could see how the projection gave its protection to a bellied-out shaft of slick, angled rock. To either side of it was the ragged, sheer face. Here it was much, much smoother and slightly angled. I began to get more and more excited.

There would be no way a person could climb up that steep slope of hard rock. Not without ropes anchored up above or plenty of time to chop ladder steps. But getting down might be another matter. A drop down that slope would not be a free fall. Not quite. At best it would be a controlled fall, slowed somewhat by friction. At the very best it would be that.

At worst . . .

At the very worst it could not be as bad as a straight drop from the handhold onto rock. It was a better chance than none.

I looked back up to that faraway handhold and was powerful glad I hadn't tried to reach it the night before. It seemed even further now than it had looked before, and I had no doubt whatever that I'd already be dead if I had tried to climb up.

I looked a long eighty feet down my rock slope and grinned to myself.

My oh my, what a little change in perspective can do to change the way a body looks at things, I thought. A week ago that slick, nearly straight up and down slope would have scared the fool out of me. Now I was looking forward to it.

Well, maybe now there was some less fool left in me than there was a week ago.

There was not much point in delaying any further. I wriggled back from the edge and—carefully—turned around. I didn't want to go over headfirst.

Talk about a worm turning. Gad, but that was uncomfortable.

The little movement I had permitted myself so far had been nothing like this. Trying to get turned around at the bottom of that uptilted projection in an area a couple feet wide and not but about a foot longer than me was no fun. It put tension on the wounds in my back and side. The blood had dried over them but they were far from starting to close. Long before I got turned I could feel a fresh flow of warm, sticky fluid softening my stiff-dried shirt and starting to spread across my back.

Every movement, every pull and tug and twist of muscle, sent fresh shoots of raw pain through every nerve in me. It was worth every bit of it.

My legs were still in fair shape and my right arm. As much as possible I held my torso stiff and did the real work with those relatively sound limbs. Even so I was weakened and dizzy from pain shock by the time I was done. But I was done. I gave a sigh of relief and started inching backward over the edge.

There was one thing I wanted to make sure of at all costs. I did not want to go sliding down that rock surface on my left side or on my back. Smooth as it was it was still hard rock. If I went down wrong it would tear the wounds open and rip them something awful. If the fall didn't kill me, and it could, I'd bleed to death inside an hour or two.

I could try to go down on my right side. It would be the most comfortable by far. That was about the only place that I didn't have some meat chunked out of me.

On the other hand that would give me very little contact with the slope surface. Very little drag to slow me down. Comfortable en route but the very devil to pay at the end of the journey.

I did not want to chance the harder impact for a little less scraping on the way down, so I swung over onto my stomach.

I had an empty, sick feeling in my stomach when I shifted back far enough for my legs to be hanging free over the edge. It was more than the lack of food. I let myself slide down a bit further, and I was committed to the slope. I knew I hadn't the strength to get back up now.

My left arm was trailing free, still on top of the projection. I looked at it but couldn't think of anything better to do with it. It wasn't as if I could lay it aside somewhere for safekeeping.

The belt holding my makeshift bandage in place low on my left side was tight against my belly. It had not occurred to me before, and it was too late to back out anyway, but I began most fervently hoping that the belt would not hang up against some irregularity on the slope.

Oh, that would be interesting. I had a vivid mental image of a sun-dried Stumpy dangling there through the years like a shriveled little advertising decoration made of tanned leather and some rag-bag pickings.

A legend would grow up around me. No doubt old Shrunken Stumpy would have been placed there as a warning. No doubt it would be known that a party of Apache warriors dried the corpse and hung it here because they thought I was trifling with the affections of a chief's beautiful, sloe-eyed daughter. Who, no doubt, I was truly in love with. And she with me.

Ah, young love. True love. I was practically weepy at the thought. The only thing disturbing me was that I don't know what a sloe-eyed girl should look like. Somehow it made me think of some sort of ugly, pig-eyed, South American wild animal instead of a pretty girl.

In years to come the local folks would drive whole coaches loaded with Eastern tourists out here to view the sight of Stumpy, the Hanging Mummy. It could become a whole new industry. Fifteen cents a trip, folks. You an' your missus both fer a quarter, sir. Step right up. Plenty of room in the coach. Watch your step, lady. An' hang onto your hats, folks. These Wild West broncs are rank. You bet.

Yeah. You bet.

And all I was doing, really, was putting off the inevitable, painful slide that would either get me on the way out of here or would get me dead a little quicker.

Either way it would be better than waiting.

I took a deep breath and shoved myself over the edge.

CHAPTER 10

I couldn't help it. A scream came tearing out of my throat when that hard, hot rock went ripping up across my stomach and chest.

The belt holding my bandanna in place against that ragged exit wound dragged against the rock and dug hard into my side, gouging deep on top of the wound. I'd felt weak before. Now I was the next thing to passing out.

I fought to stay aware of what I was doing, to keep my legs and my one good arm splayed out against the slope to drag and to slow my fall as much as possible. I could not afford to tumble free and roll to the bottom.

I gathered speed quickly, too quickly, and the slope was a gray curtain that rushed past my eyes. Once without thinking I let my neck relax. My head sagged forward and my chin bounced off the stone. My teeth clacked together sharply, and I knew I had left some skin on the rough surface.

The only good thing about that sliding fall was that it could not last long. At the time it seemed forever, but I know it could not have been more than scant seconds from when I let go of my hold at the top and when I hit piled sand at the bottom.

I felt my feet plunge into the sand drift. They stopped short and my body, still falling, was suddenly jackknifed. I knew I was being thrown backward by the impact. My head snapped forward when I doubled over at the waist, and the quick stabbing pain in my back and side was cut off by a loud, dull thump that I heard more than felt against my forehead. Mercifully, I felt no more.

When I came around it was slowly. There was a sense of great lassitude within me. I felt warm and greatly at peace. My thoughts floated pleasantly apart from my body. Had the Trask boys come upon me then I believe I would have smiled with benign good will while they unlimbered their revolvers and tripped the triggers.

That thought came to me, and I agreed with it. It seemed a nice idea. It would please them. It would not displease me. There was something mildly wrong about the idea, and vaguely I wondered what it might be.

I was puzzled by the dim sense of wrongness and I began lazily to pursue the question. Then, like tumblers falling in a lock, my emotions and physical senses and capacity for rational thought returned. And I was frightened. By myself and by that lapse of will more than by any external threat.

I was lying on my back, half rolled onto my right side in deep sand. My head was turned at an awkward angle to the right, and my right arm—my good arm—felt dead. The whole left side of my neck felt afire from the strain of being forced askew for so long. I seemed to be lying on a downhill slant and part of my weight had been held by my head and neck. When I raised my head I slid several inches further.

I tried to sit up and at first could not. Neither arm wanted to respond. I twisted and wriggled, trying to ignore the sheets of pain that came from the bullet wounds, and slithered another foot or two until I was lying sideways at the foot of the sand drift with good, hard earth beneath me.

Putting the effort on my stomach muscles, I sat up and tried not to feel the dull red heat in my neck. I looked at my right arm and could see nothing wrong. I made a fist and the fingers responded.

Ten thousand needles jammed themselves deep into the flesh of that arm, and I cried out. But it was as much in relief as in discomfort. The arm had been deadened by my weight. With the flow of blood restored, feeling came back. And movement. Each prickling wave of feeling with each succeeding motion became a joy.

I grinned and lurched to my feet. It was painful. It was worth it.

I stood, weak and swaying and dizzy. But I stood. On solid ground. I was battered, shot, my clothes torn to rags and caked hard with dried blood and dirt. But I stood. I was free. I was alive.

I took a single, tottering step. And another. I did not mind the pain at all. It was beautiful, grand. I liked being alive to feel it. I took another step forward. Toward the south. Toward the water that I knew would be there.

I have no idea of how many times I stumbled during that endless journey of several miles nor of how many times I fell. All that I remember with clarity is the cold, biting feel of water on my face and the cleansing, life-giving feel of it going down my throat. That and the bright, savage sense of satisfaction that I had reached this distant goal.

In the past I had known anger. I had known the desire for revenge. I had known the heat of the gun-wish.

I had never known this feeling before.

Now I know what it is that gleams like unholy light behind the eyes of a hunting wolf. It is the absolute and unhurried certainty that before the run is ended he will drink the blood of his prey.

I drank of that water and it had the taste of blood and I was glad. I had no doubts now. No thing and no person would halt me now. There was neither doubt nor urgency within me.

I slept.

CHAPTER 11

There was a wood pole suspended across in front of my chest and I looked at it and was mildly curious about how it had come to be there. As long as it was, I couldn't go any further. I had to keep going forward. I didn't remember why.

I couldn't keep on just standing there. My knees were buckling, and I worked my legs up and down like I was treading on something at the bottom of a barrel. It seemed to help for a while. I reached out to take hold of the peeled log for support but it was too late. I went down and only just managed to hook an arm over the second of three rails.

There were some shoes on the ground below my eyes, and something took hold under my chin and tilted my head back. There was a brown, wrinkled face close above mine and dark whiskers shot through with white hairs. He had a tobacco stain in his beard at the right corner of his mouth.

I groped for a name to go with that face, and it came to me. Maxfield, the name was. He had something to do with horses. And a mule. My mule.

I knew where I was then. The town. Friendly. And Miss Janet was here. It was all right now.

Maxfield was saying something, and I concentrated hard to make out the meaning of the sounds.

"Wolf. Wolf," he kept saying, over and over again. It made no sense.

Then it did. He was saying, "Wolfe." It was the name Miss Janet had given me here. He was talking to me. I tried to say something back, but the words did not come out. They formed in my mind but not in my throat.

"Hogan," Maxfield hollered. "Come here quick."

Maxfield knelt beside me. He smelled of strong soap and corn whiskey. He draped my left arm across his shoulders and I winced at renewed pain in my side. Then Hogan was there, and my right arm was lifted.

Supporting me between them, they dragged me across an expanse of packed earth, up a step, and across a broad stoop. We went through a doorway into cool darkness. It was the first I'd been inside a house in quite some time.

They stretched me out on a bed. The ropes creaked and sagged and for one panicky instant I thought they would not hold. My muscles contracted in alarm, and I cried out from the pain that caused.

"Lay easy now, Mr. Wolfe. You're all right now."

"Look here, Glen. He's been shot. Sure enough, he has."

"Hmm, yes. It wasn't that old mule, anyway. I would have felt some blame if he'd been stomped."

"What happened, Wolfe?"

I had some difficulty focusing my eyes, Hogan had a worried expression.

I tried on a smile to see how it felt for a change and croaked out, "Jus' lucky, I guess."

Hogan shook his head. He lifted me up some and Maxfield held something to my lips. He tilted the bottle and a fine, rich flavor flooded my mouth. When it hit bottom I could feel the spreading warmth that comes from good whiskey.

"Hope you know . . . I'm obliged," I said. It was some easier to talk this time.

"Could you use a bite to eat?" Maxfield asked.

"Uh-huh. Anything . . . from hog slops upward."

He seemed pleased with the idea of feeding someone. He bobbed his head and disappeared.

Hogan laid me back down on the bed and set about stripping away what was left of my clothes. He sort of sucked his lips in against his teeth at what all he saw, but he didn't say anything. I guessed it was a good thing I couldn't see too.

The bandanna he had to soak with water to get loose. It was

stuck to that exit wound. I was some relieved when the job was done. Not just to have it over with. Mostly to not be smelling the sick-sweet stench of rotting meat that goes with gangrene. Most any clean wound will heal itself in the dry, clean air of the high country if you just give it a bit of time without being disturbed. It was the hole in my side that had fretted me. It seemed the danger was worst with ragged wounds where living blood might not get to all the torn flesh. I had been lucky, I knew.

Hogan cut away my clothes rather than roll me around too much. They were not worth trying to save at this point.

My gunbelt and money belt he laid in reach of my hand. Then he took a bit of rag and used some of Maxfield's white whiskey to dab at my side and three places on my back. It stung, and proper too, but it was no worse than I had been feeling.

"Someone done a pretty fair job on you, Wolfe," he said.

"He did try hard," I told him. "Does Mi . . . Does my cousin know I'm here?"

He grunted what might have been disgust or might have been just an exclamation about his own forgetfulness. "That's right. You wouldn't know, would you?"

"Reckon I don't."

"Well, she ain't here. Left a couple days ago." I waited for him to go on. "Your mule came home a couple days ago. Four days, it would o' been. She got all excited. Had Glen drive her into Apishapa City."

I raised an eyebrow at him.

"He got the wheel fixed for his wagon. Jerry fin'ly got it done for him. An' Glen, he took the lady where she wanted to go. Just got back las' night."

I assumed Jerry was the blacksmith and fix-it man I hadn't seen before. Nor this time either. And Miss Janet had taken off on her own. To the same place where I'd told the Trask boys she would be. I'd had no idea she would ever set foot in the town when I told them. But still . . .

For just an instant I thought about trying to get up. But it was no use even thinking about. I would not be going anywhere for a while. I let myself go loose on that soft indoors bed and it was a relief not having to try and get out of it right away.

Before long Maxfield was there again. He had a bowl in his hand that turned out to contain dried beef that'd been mashed into a powder and mixed in with a whole can of condensed milk. That mixture of his didn't taste like much but it was plenty rich and seemed to hold half the world's supply of quick nourishment. I did feel better after the two of them had spooned it into me.

When I was done I never had time to so much as say thank you. I closed my eyes and went off sound asleep.

I spent five days laying up in Glen Maxfield's bed, most of that time listening to him talk. Maxfield, it turned out, was a man with too few people who would listen to him, and I suppose all the folks in Friendly had heard all of his stories several times over.

As I'd suspected before, at heart he was a dirt farmer. He'd had one lone, adventuresome impulse in his life—though he didn't say it quite that way—and had sold a piece of rich Iowa cropland to come west and raise him some dogies. He'd started a little herd at that time a few years ago when running beef had the glitter of gold for anyone who owned so much as two cows and a bull. And he'd got started just in time for the big die-up of '86, right on the heels of the big price plunge. He must have been one of the very last men who'd paid big for stock cows.

Since then he'd stayed put, swapping a few horses and tending a garden and, I think, wishing there was water enough that he could hitch his team to a plow and roll some grass under in favor of grain.

I came to admire the man, though. In all his talk and with all the ill luck he'd had, Maxfield never once had a note of whine in his voice.

When he told me of it, it was with a chuckle over his own stupidity. There was no bitterness in him nor the least trace of self-pity.

We talked for long hours, whenever I was awake, though it was always made plain that I should fade off to sleep any time I would or could. And while we talked he kept me full of coffee and his odd but health-giving beef soup and an occasional cup of his good corn. After a couple days he added red meat to the diet, and I found that he'd at least picked up on some of the best of the cowman's habits. He fixed me thick slabs of fresh beef, fried in a skillet that ran deep with beef tallow, and for a late meal treat he'd pour us each a dish of the piping hot tallow and mix some molasses into it. We'd spoon it up quick before the tallow cooled and laugh when it gummed to the roofs of our mouths.

I rubbed my stomach and sat back in the chair he'd finally allowed me to sit in. "You can cook, Glen. Better than any trail cook I ever come across."

"I'm a better nurse than a cook. You're starting to mend, I'd say. The wounds have stopped draining now."

"Yes."

"I expect you've been thinking of leaving."

"Yes."

He shook his head. "It is too soon for riding."

"I've been laying here too long already. I can use my left arm all right now. I can shove my hand in my belt to keep from putting any strain on it, and I'll be fine."

"Sure," he said, but his tone made plain that he did not believe it.

"Look, Glen . . ." I hesitated, unsure of how to go on.

"Don't be saying it."

"Well, I will say thank you. It was a decent and a generous thing you've done for me."

"No more than was right. And that is enough talk of it."

I nodded and was glad to call an end to the conversation. It was embarrassing for some reason, although it should not have been.

I stood and was pleased to find that while my legs felt weak they were steady enough. "I'd better take a look at the mule."

Maxfield was at the door before me. "You'll find him in good shape. Better than you, to be sure."

We walked to the corral, Maxfield keeping the pace deliberately slow. He was a considerate man as well as a kind one.

The late afternoon sun was warm on my face, the first I had felt in days, and a fresh breeze felt even better. It was a relief to be able to look upward to open sky and far distances again. The ground we walked on seemed far away but it was good to have it there.

The mule was in the same enclosure where I had first seen him, and from the condition of his coat and the fat over his ribs it was obvious that Maxfield had been taking as good care of the mount as he had the master.

My beat-up old saddle hull and trappings were slung over a staub of rail under cover of the shed roof. It looked as though the leather had been oiled since I saw it last.

We stopped at the fence and Gray stood with his head down, not obvious about the attention he was giving us but with an ear cocked in our direction. But then I had not been enough in his company for any bond to develop between us.

Maxfield's two heavy horses whickered to him and came to the fence to thrust inquisitive muzzles toward their owner. The rough string of would-be saddle horses milled in a tight knot at the far end of the corral, churning the earth into dust beneath nervous hooves. I was more glad than ever that I had not settled for one of that lot.

"He seems steady enough," Maxfield said, looking at the mule. He stood with one large-knuckled hand scratching at the hollow behind the left ear of one of his huge geldings. The animal had a placid, woozy-eyed look about it. It stretched its muzzle to nestle affectionately in his armpit. "You don't really have to go at all, you know," he said casually. "After whoever it was shot you, I mean."

"Uh-huh. I know."

Oh, I had thought about it. In many ways Maxfield was perfectly right. I didn't really *have* to go hobbling and limping off to Apishapa City like a broken-winged rooster bent on some ludicrous form of revenge. Instead I could lay back in Glen Maxfield's house, enjoy his company and good cooking until the last scab peeled away, and then ride off on my own business. In a direction exactly opposite that of Apishapa City.

I mean, I *did* have business to tend to with a Mormon rancher over on the Utah side of the high mountains. It was where I'd

been going when all this started and I shared Miss Janet's fire unexpected and got more trouble than I needed or would have
looked for.

It wasn't as if any of this was really my problem. I suppose I
should have been happy to count myself well out of it. Gather up
the reins of that mule and point his nose toward Utah. Those
long, strong legs of his would put me there in a week or a little
more. There was no good reason not to do it. No one was waiting
for me in Apishapa City. No one was counting on me for help.
Miss Janet had even made something of a point of *not* asking for
old Stumpy's help. In fact she hadn't been real anxious to be bur-
dened with me. She'd made it pretty plain that to her I was just a
peon, something passed along the byway and worth no more notice than a sheep or a steer. Able to feed and fend for itself in
some limited way but of no large value. Certainly neither an ally
nor a confidant. No, it was clear she would not be waiting for me
anywhere nor counting on me in any way.

On the other hand, that Mormon wasn't expecting me at any
particular time. Sometime before the fall roundup, was all. It sure
made no difference to his beeves. Like the old joke says, what's
time to a cow?

Back there behind me somewhere the two remaining Trask
boys would still be in pursuit of that girl—maybe had fetched up
with her by now—knowing that they'd left me dead behind them.

Well, I sort of hate to give anyone a wrong impression. It
doesn't seem honest somehow. And those boys had a wrong idea
about my health. I wouldn't mind correcting them.

They had shot down that ugly old horse of mine, and worthless
as he was I still wanted to discuss that with them.

They had laid in ambush to shoot me down and when I gave all
appearances of being down and done for had put another bullet
in my back. It was a thing they should be admonished about.
Definitely not a socially acceptable form of conduct. It should be
discussed.

And there was Miss Janet. A pretty little child-woman, she was,
but I had no idea what was in her head nor even what it was the
Trasks wanted of her. She was fearful of them, and I did not even

know why. After all that had happened to me, I had no faint idea of why. Nor had I any idea of what might have happened to the girl since I saw her last.

She had reached the town, that I knew. There could be safety there for her if only she would go to the authorities and ask their help. The town marshal, the county sheriff, or simply the towns-people. No one would permit a woman to be molested. Not as long as they could pull a trigger. Decent women, even not so de-cent ones, were regarded as being beyond the reach of violence, and anyone who thought otherwise was asking for some kind of big trouble. The Trask boys might not know that. They would find out quickly if only Miss Janet let her troubles be known.

The big question was, would she?

Somehow I did not think she had nor that she would.

It would have been simple for her to ask for protection when we first reached Friendly. It would have taken no more than a word, and surely she knew that. The least hint of her trouble would have brought a flock of deputies to Friendly with a holiday-happy posse behind them.

Yet she had not given that word. Instead she had prepared that cock-and-bull tale about us being cousins who'd managed to lose our transportation somewhere along the way.

She hadn't said anything about the truth. I could not under-stand why. It must have been a compelling reason. She seemed a fairly sensible girl. She must have had some good reason. Some-thing I could not know about.

But if that reason existed then, it probably existed now. And so I expected she would still be trying to handle things her own way. It was a thought to make me shudder. The Trask boys would like it just fine.

So all right. I was worried about the girl. After all, I was the dumb-dumb who'd pointed the Trasks her way. And I was curious about her. And I had something of a score to settle with the boys. And . . . maybe part of it was that I was still some piqued about her condescending attitude toward me. Maybe I wanted to tell her she should look at a man as a man and not as some faceless peasant. Maybe that had something to do with it too, to be honest about it. Maybe that had a lot to do with it. I did not try to understand why that should be important to me. I don't think I wanted to know.

I thought about it and knew I was not even tempted by the idea of slipping quietly out a back door. The man in Utah could wait awhile. And Miss Janet . . .

Maxfield coughed politely and brought me back to the real world with something of a start. I had been staring out to the far mountains but seeing nothing. Or perhaps a piece of everything.

He gave the big, docile gelding a final pat on the side of its thick, crested neck and turned toward the house. "Better get some rest if you're leaving tomorrow."

"Yeah." We walked back slowly. It seemed a long and tiring distance.

CHAPTER 12

The mule walked, head bobbing up and down in the slow, dogged rhythm that could go on for so long without pause. It was not endurance I wanted from him, though. It was steadiness. It was minimal shock, a lessening of the fire that spread with each jolt or jar. I was healing. I was not yet healed. The riding hurt and there was no denying it.

Friendly to Apishapa City. Sixty miles, they'd said. A brisk half day for a mount and rider in good condition. A full day for a family in a gig for a trip into town. Me it had already taken all of yesterday and I was still a couple miles out.

I suppose I could have pushed on in the night before, but it would have been uncomfortable at best. And I wanted to be reasonably fresh when I arrived. The Trasks might be there, and if so they would have had about a week to ingratiate themselves with the people of the town. Pleasant and likeable boys that they were.

From two miles out the town lay before me, spread out at the base of a long and gentle slope. It was a splash of white against a dark green line of foliage. The green, I knew, would be cottonwoods and wild plum and elderberries. Hidden somewhere beneath it would be the bed of the stream that someone had dignified by calling it a river. It would be nearly dry at this time of year. That would not matter. The river would still be of comfort to the town. It gave the town a reason for its placement and a promise of sweet, rushing water in the spring. Perhaps more important it gave them trees and shade and some semblance of green beauty amid the sere and arid landscape around them. It would be a good place to live and I had no doubt that the townspeople took considerable pride in their community.

We came closer, the mule's freshly shod hooves raising small puffs of dust that hung above the road surface behind us. I cannot pretend that I was not nervous. I was not in the best of condition. There was no way I could stand up to either of the Trask boys in a toe-to-toe brawl. Worse, I was not at all certain that I was in condition to face them with a gun. If my reflexes had been slowed . . .

I forced myself away from that train of thought. Next to the physical possession of a revolver or rifle or shotgun, the most important weapon a man can have in a gunfight is confidence in himself. And if I didn't have much right now there was no point in dumping away any that I did have.

We passed a few outlying homes and what appeared to be a small dairy. Some twenty-odd milch cows shifted slowly around a hay bunk. They were sleek creatures of some Channel Islands bloodline, I guessed, with their abnormally high hipbones and weighty, balloon-like udders. I suppose these animals have a right and proper place for the service of man. But I could not learn to love them in the way that I love the wild and free—if uneconomical—long-horned Texas beeves.

The outlying buildings thickened until the gray mule and I no longer rode on a country road but were on a town street with white-painted fences and tiny front porches and neat little hand-tended, hand-watered gardens in the side yards. As we neared the town center and the river course there were shade trees in the yards as well. The air that seeped from under these trees was cool and was lightly scented with a delicate leaf smell. It came welcome to nostrils unaccustomed to more than earth and sun-dried brush and animal sweat, my own included.

A courthouse, spire capped and imposing, stood beside the barren creek bed, and around it on three sides away from the river were tidy rows of shops and respectable businesses, each with a plank walk laid before it. Stout rails and decorative hitching posts were placed along the walks, and on the street sides surrounding the courthouse were public troughs. I headed first for one of these.

Gray sank his muzzle deep into the water in a low cast-iron trough. His ears twitched back with each swallow, and as always it made me think of those ears as a pump handle somehow being used to pull the water up to the throat passage. I just plain like to watch a horse or a mule drink. It always tickles me. Silly maybe, but true.

Now that I'd arrived I began wondering what I should do next. I could go blustering about, asking for Miss Janet and generally making a nuisance of myself. It would be a good way to call attention to myself. Of course I didn't know what name Miss Janet would be using here, darn her. Come to think of it, maybe her name wasn't Janet Cates either. It was sure that her name wasn't Wolfe any more than my name was. She could have decided to use any name here.

Or I could go stomping around asking for the Trasks. If they were here they'd had plenty of time to establish themselves as good old boys. And if that was so, they would likely be directed to me before I would be shown to them. I sure had no illusions about those nice boys versus the morality of back-shooting.

So all right. I would just wander around and see what I could see. I led Gray across the wide, rutted street that formed one side of the town square and tied him to a post where he wouldn't be bothered by other animals like at a common rail. For the most part horses get along well with mules, but you never know, and I sure didn't want to jump into the middle of an equine rib-thumping contest.

There was a barber pole standing on the walk at the far end of the block, and it seemed a likely place to listen to some conversation. I walked down that way, passing some shops with women's foofaraw in the windows and an ice-cream parlor with some ladies inside and some men who wore fresh collars over their ties and kept their coats on whilst the ladies were present.

When I got to the barbershop I seen that it catered to the same class of trade. With my looks and wearing stiff new range clothes from Hogan's shelves back in Friendly—my old outfit had been ruined entire—I was apt to present a suspicious appearance, and I did not want that. I walked past the open door of the barbershop without slowing and stopped on the street corner to think for a minute.

There was bound to be another barber chair in a less respectable part of town, and there would certainly be some saloons where they'd take my money. But then again, those Trask boys did not shape up as being the rough-and-ready cowhand type of traveler. It took no special talent to figure that when they hit town it would be the banker and the lawyers and the better grade of businessmen they'd want to drink with. I would get nowhere or at the very best would move a lot slower if I spent my time listening to people who'd only seen them pass at a distance.

I took a look around and spotted a haberdasher's storefront sign on the far side of the square, so I ambled over that way. The storekeeper did not seem overjoyed when I entered, but he got over that pretty soon. With his kind assistance, and a deep dip into my money belt, I managed to put up a respectable front.

When I hit the street again I felt like a fair bully gent my own self. I had on a new suit of dark gray broadcloth with the shelf creases helpfully ironed out on the spot. I had a dark blue vest with an imitation gold chain strung across my belly and a fresh shirt with a stiff and sparkly white celluloid collar. I hadn't been willing to part with my boots, but they were fresh blacked and greased to a high gloss. And on my head was a spanking new John B. Stetson, a stockman's hat with the little three-inch brim that would never do for riding in the far lonesome under sun and rain. A pretty thing it was, too, in a light, silver belly color. My riding clothes were rolled in a bundle and tied with twine. I strapped them behind my saddle, took a moment to scuff the toes of my boots, and headed back toward the barbershop.

I hung my hat and coat on a deerhorn rack and nodded to the other four men in the shop. There were two men sitting in rocking chairs where they could look out the front window, one fellow in the high work chair and another doing the cutting. They'd stopped talking when I walked in, and I tried to look as agreeable as possible when I nodded to them.

"Good morning," I said, careful not to let the g sluff off at the end of the word.

"Mornin'," the barber said. "Be with you directly."

"I'm in no special hurry." I sat in an empty rocker close to the other customers but separated from them by a vacant chair. There was a copy of that week's local newspaper on the caned chair seat and I picked it up to browse through while I got on with my eavesdropping.

The paper seemed a prosperous enough journal. There were front page advertisements for a feed mill, a harness shop, two general mercantile establishments, and one for a sporting goods dealer offering an end-of-summer stock reduction sale on all baseball equipment. There was bound to be a men's league organized in the town and maybe a semiprofessional team as well. I chuckled to myself and thought about all the impassioned pleas that advertisement would have caused among small but aspiring boys on all sides of the town.

Directly the other waiting customers resumed their talk, and I listened with one ear and read with one eye and was content enough.

My two neighbors seemed to be lawyers. They were discussing some farmer's water rights claim up the river and trying to guess how Uncle Orville would rule. Uncle Orville, I took it, was a judge hereabouts. I guessed that the title Uncle was a term of affectionate respect and not indicative of some familial ties among the town's legal practitioners.

The telegraph news service reported that Cleveland was standing heavily on the gold standard in his campaign for re-election. The editor made it clear that this was not popular in a Colorado rich with low value silver. At the state level there was talk of extending the vote to women, perhaps during the next session of the legislature. From South Dakota it was reported that fears about another outbreak of Ghost Dancers among the Indians were just a rumor and that farmers did not have to worry about another spate of trouble on the reservations.

Maybe not, I thought. I didn't know much about Indians on up to the north country. But there were still a good many places where I wouldn't want to be riding without a gun close to hand. Not that I was a fanatic on the subject. More like healthily cautious and maybe a bit skeptical about government assurances that just because there's no big trouble it means there isn't any trouble at all. Somehow I can't expect any man to roll over and play dead just because he's supposed to have been on the losing end of something. I guess the Indians had their own point of view on things and regardless of what the tribes said, there would be individual resentments hanging on for a long, long time.

Not that there should be much to worry about around here. The Navaho had been peaceful so long that people tended to forget they'd once been as handy with a knife as they were now with a pair of sheep shears.

I read along and kept listening. One of the lawyers was talking about getting up a party to head for the mountains on an elk hunt and maybe after some bear.

"I could use a good rug for my office," the other said, "and elk meat is quite pleasant."

"So I've been told. Are they hard to kill?"

"Not really. They will be coming down from their summer range soon. You just wait for a fat cow to pass and use a heavy bullet. It is an experience you should have."

"I would like to get a good head. Ship it back to my father for the wall of his study. I think it would please him."

"The court docket is rather open for the next month. I don't think we would be losing much if we spent that time in the field. No reason why you can't collect a good head and still put a cow in the smokehouse for winter."

"Done," the first one said quickly. He sounded elated by the prospect, and I tried to remember how long it had been since I'd felt that same anticipation of sport afield. A long while.

I kept my head down to the paper but I almost missed the news item tucked decently away on the fourth of six pages.

Mr. Benjamin Trask, late of Pueblo County, wishes to express his appreciation to the townspeople and officers of the court of Apishapa City, for their kindnesses in securing treatment for his unfortunate sister, Miss Janet Cates Trask. Mr. Trask has expressed interest in securing lands within the jurisdiction of this County for investment purposes and with the object of providing citizens with a School Lands preserve for the ultimate establishment of a publicly owned Normal School for young ladies. Residents of the County are urged to open their hearts to so generous a young man as he has proven himself to be.

My oh my, I did think to myself. A normal school. What a thoughtful boy, that Benjamin. Now was he proposing this in memory of his late, lamented sister? Or in her honor? The mention of court officers made things quite unclear.

But there were ways to find out.

"Oh, this *is* bully," I mused aloud. "Think of the effect a normal school will have on the community."

"I beg your pardon?"

I looked up, contriving to look startled and more than a little sheepish. I smiled at the lawyers. "I *am* sorry. I was muttering aloud again. Disreputable habit, that. It is just that I was so impressed by the city when I arrived, and I notice in the newspaper that you are to have a normal school here. What a delightful prospect. Tremendous opportunity for growth."

"You are a land speculator, sir?" He sounded wary. No doubt he had seen my range clothes when I walked past the first time.

"Oh no," I said with a cheery wave of one hand. "Merely an observation on the good fortune of your city. I'm a cattle buyer myself. My speculating is strictly in livestock values per hundredweight at the far end versus hoof values at the buying end. Wouldn't know enough about farmland to buy or sell it honestly nor enough about the law to do it dishonestly, so I have to leave both to the other fellow."

It drew a sharp snort of laughter from my lawyer friend. His companion smiled and was about to say something when the barber dismissed his haircut victim and summoned the fellow to the tall chair. I did not at all mind being left alone with the first counselor.

"If you continue to attract such civic-minded folk as this," I said with a tap against the newspaper, "Apishapa City will be making a fine name for itself. You already seem to have a fine town, sir. Solid community. Place where a man can raise his children."

"Indeed we do, sir." He leaned forward and extended his hand. "Louis Farley, sir. Attorney at law."

"James D. Williams of Tilden, Texas, sir, and glad to make your acquaintance." I regretted that as soon as I said it, but of course by then it was too late. What would a Texas cattle buyer be doing in Colorado when there was a virtual sea of marketable beef between there and here? I'd spoken from habit since it was the simple truth. Not that it appeared to matter. Farley gave no indication that he found it odd.

"Are you looking to buy beeves here then, Mr. Williams?"

"No, sir, I am not at the moment. Merely marking time, waiting wire confirmation of a bank credit from Chicago, then I will travel north. I understand there will be a herd available there at an *exceptionally* good value. Dissolution of partnership, I understand." I hoped that would help cover my mistake.

Farley smiled. We understood each other quite nicely, thank you. I was of a class suitable for casual conversation and perhaps a few rounds of poker. There was no immediate prospect of his making money from me, but neither was I threatening to take any out of his reach. It bade well for a pleasant relationship.

"As a buyer, Mr. Williams, what do you think of the improved strains of beef cattle?" Meaning, as a lawyer he had got ownership of at least a piece of someone's beef herd. And more than likely his partner was someone who was either old-fashioned enough to be resisting the new blood or was someone young and eager enough to be rejecting the old and durable range breed completely.

"The improved strains, the Durham and more particularly the new Hereford, give a better carcass weight. Packing houses will pay a premium for them, but of course the rancher expects a premium price as well. From my point of view one may often more than offset the other. There is still money to be made with the old body type. Personally I like to see a good infusion of the new blood." I smiled. "But not so much that the producer demands an excessive premium."

He liked that, could appreciate it quite well. We talked on, about livestock for the most part. I had already disclaimed knowledge of the law. And I wondered desperately how I could turn the conversation back to Benjamin Trask the Benefactor and his unfortunate sister, recently given such kind aid by the townspeople and the court officers of Apishapa City.

We talked. Another customer came in and settled himself behind a barricade of full-bodied beard. Behind me another came to the door, turned, and left without entering. Too much business turns away business, I supposed.

My new friend took his turn in the barber's chair, and I was left without a point of entry to the conversation I wanted.

I need not have bothered worrying about it.

I sat luxuriating in the feel of a hot towel around my face. It felt marvelously refreshing.

Which, in retrospect, was marvelously nice. When the barber removed the towel I was looking at two tall, badge-wearing, gun-in-hand gentlemen. And the Brothers Trask. Good Benjamin on my left. Helpful Tom on my right.

I could not say the surprise was a joyous one. Total, yes. Pleasant, no.

"That is the man, Marshal," Ben said. He pointed an accusing finger at me. The marshal pointed a somewhat more threatening revolver at me.

"How do, Benny," I said. I held my hands well out to the sides and smiled. "What can I do for you, boys?"

CHAPTER 13

I got the impression that the marshal—his name was Dave French—would have been a likeable and most agreeable person under other circumstances. As it was, he worked real hard at making sure no taint of humane consideration crept through in his treatment of me. It would not do for the good people of Apishapa City to think their marshal was going soft on such a totally despicable, loathsome, and more than likely deranged creature as was currently housed in his jail.

After all, wasn't he dealing with the kind of scrum who'd (blush) taken physical advantage of that poor, feeble-minded Trask girl when she was lost out on the desert? Before she'd turned up here under some delusion that her name was Wolfe? Before her worried-sick brothers came along and found her? Before young Benjamin produced a court judgment entered in Pueblo County attesting to the girl's feeble-mindedness and placing her under the protective guardianship of her uncle?

And what could have been more natural than for her loving brothers to protect the child by refraining from previous mention of the carnal assault on her virtue. They had never dreamed that this low creature could ever be found in the open wastelands of the western United States.

Now that he had so unexpectedly surfaced it was clearly their duty—for the sake of protecting other innocent womenfolk—to expose the foul beast.

Good of them, I was sure. Not that I took too happily to the thought of the way people looked at me when they came into the marshal's office on some pretext so they could view the caged beast. Or to the penchant they had, grown men as well as the expected small boys, for throwing garbage and horse apples and other smelly oddments through my cell window.

Well, at least I knew what had happened to Miss Janet. It did not help for me to know I had led the boys to her.

And I suppose I could not greatly blame the marshal. He was young for the job, about in his early twenties. He had not been at it long enough to work out a reliable sameness in the matter of handling prisoners. He would not yet be sure enough of his own manhood to ignore detractors or to stop looking for imagined ones. I could understand his attitude even if I could not actually sympathize with it.

He was dutiful enough, I will say that for him. And someday he could make a fair to middling peace officer.

The law says that an accused person has the right to be informed of the charges placed against him. He told me that himself. And about all the accusations and explanations that led to my arrest.

He told me several times, in fact. Speaking slowly and in an overly loud voice, enunciating each word carefully, individually. I think he believed that in this way he could penetrate the dark mists that must surely have been shifting and swirling within my defective brain.

And I'd thought I had been treated like a village idiot before. I hadn't had the half of it then.

Unfortunately Marshal French's zeal for meeting the letter of the law stopped somewhere short of giving the accused a chance to speak in his own defense. Every time I tried to open my mouth to say something he would start hollering. When I was aggravatingly persistent about it he would call a deputy to stand by with drawn and cocked revolver while French tried to batter some sense into me.

I guess he accomplished his goal, at that. After a couple days I learned to keep my mouth shut.

On the fourth day, Ben came to visit me. I heard him telling French he thought he might be able to trick a confession out of me if he was given a little time alone with me.

To give the marshal his due, I will say that he took Ben's gun, made sure the office gun cabinet was locked, and left me and Ben on opposite sides of the cell door before he took his leave. No one was going to kill off his most sensational prisoner before he'd had a chance to parade me in a court of law.

As soon as French was out of hearing Ben padded over to the cell door and gave me a bright, happy grin.

"You certainly gave poor Tom a fright when he saw you in that barbershop, Stumpy. We thought sure you had been digested by the buzzards before then."

"Your concern for your brother overwhelms me, Benjamin."

His eyes hardened and there was no trace of false gaiety left on his face. "He's the only brother I have left, you know."

"No, I didn't as a matter of fact, but it is a good thing to remember. It helps to keep track of how many Trasks I need to speak to in the future."

"You don't have any future, cowboy."

I shrugged. "Maybe. But I don't expect to quit hopin'."

"You know, Williams, I could almost want you to wiggle out of this somehow. I would really like to finish you with my own hands. I would enjoy that."

I forced a laugh. "Why Benny-boy, I'll be happy to accept any help you want to give me. I could even suggest a thing or two."

There was hate in Ben's eyes, and I welcomed it. For once again I felt that deep, sure, blood knowledge. It rose from somewhere within me and I found myself working my jaw, impatient for the taste of bright, flowing blood.

It must have shown on my face because Ben's normally tanned, even features turned white. He took a step backward, then caught himself. He flushed a red as bright as the whiteness had been pale and turned to hurry out through the front door of Marshal French's tidy little brick jail. He did not even have the presence of mind to claim he had extracted his confession from me. A most unseemly error on his part.

I wondered briefly why he had come. Just for the pleasure of gloating over his very own, personal prisoner, I finally decided. For in spite of what the marshal and the townspeople might think, I was Ben Trask's prisoner. The other people in the town were just his tools in the matter.

My big problem was trying to find a way to turn that situation around. A most difficult undertaking—nasty word, that—when I was not allowed to so much as speak to anyone.

My first obvious step was to establish communications with someone. With anyone, no matter how hostile, except for Ben or Tom Trask.

Then what? Well, I didn't rightly know about that. There would sure be no point in asking anyone to check the boys' story with Miss Janet. She was a certified lunatic as far as this town knew. With court papers to prove it, regardless of how Ben might have obtained a judge's ruling on the subject. And that was something I didn't even *want* to know.

I couldn't turn to Glen Maxfield for help in explaining the true story. Oh, I could prove easy enough that I'd been beat and shot and otherwise made to feel unloved. But I couldn't prove who'd done it, nor could Maxfield. He could only say what condition I'd been in when I stumbled into Friendly that second time.

Worse, much worse, Glen Maxfield thought all along that my name was Thomas Wolfe. The same name Miss Janet had been using here in Apishapa City before her sort-of brothers got her locked up.

I mean, Ben was a very quick boy with his brain and no stranger to fast lying. He would not be one to miss the damaging possibilities in that name business. I could just imagine the way he'd turn that to his own advantage.

"Think of that, neighbor. Doesn't that disgust you? Doesn't that *prove* that this low animal, this unspeakably vile creature approaching my poor, dear sister, that poor child without the wits, without the God-given intelligence to defend herself from such monsters, does not this *prove* that he actually convinced that poor girl that she was his wife and used that cruel and awful lie to force himself upon her? And in such a cunning fashion that the innocent, feeble-minded victim of his scheme would not then report him to the proper authorities. Yes, neighbor, there is your proof. *Proof* of his evil intent. Well, I am not ashamed to say that I am

grateful. Yes, grateful. Grateful that there are still good and honest and decent people in this world who care enough to protect
the innocent from people, nay from beasts, such as this Stumpy
Williams. Yes, neighbor, thanks to your diligence, thanks to your
concern, your humanity, this monster will threaten innocent girls
no more. Thanks to you, neighbor, my sister and your daughter
will be safe in their beds tonight."

I'll bet that's just the pitch old Benjamin would have used.
There was sure no point in looking to Maxfield for help.

Of course, none of it would make any difference if I couldn't
even get anyone to listen to me. They didn't even let me say
thank you when I got fed twice a day—and without so much as a
spoon for an eating tool at that.

I thought on it considerable and paced around some in my six-
by-eight cell and peered out the barred cell window for a while.
I'd have settled for a jailbreak lickety-split if I'd had the chance,
but of course I didn't. Jail builders are not too awful stupid as a
rule, and the fellow who'd built this one did good work.

The bars on the door and the window were high quality steel
set deep in sturdy brick construction. You could have wrapped a
log chain on any one of those bars, hitched an elephant to it and
got no more result than to wear some harness galls on the elephant's shoulders.

There was no lock on the cell door to even try picking. It was
fastened shut by an arrangement of sliding steel bars controlled
with a lever. The lever was on the other side of a brick wall, inside
a locked case. No way to reach it.

The only thing I had in there with me was a rope-sprung bunk,
and even there the builder had been smart. There was no metal
anywhere in that contraption. No nails or bolts that might have
been used to chip or scrape at the mortar in the walls. The frame
was pegged with wood dowels. Even the rope support for the
straw mattress was made of many lengths of light cord. Plenty of
it but hardly any strength in it. And French had taken away everything I'd owned with any metal in it, right down to my nailed-sole
boots.

I went to the window again. There was not much to see. A

trash-strewn alley and the board and batten side of the building next door. As usual there were a couple small boys lurking among the trash bins with piles of horse manure close to hand. Every so often one would try to pitch a clod of dung through the cell window, especially if I stood too close to the window so they could see me there. Then there was a veritable barrage of horse apples flying through the air.

I thought, and couldn't help but grin at the idea, that at least I was making a contribution to this community. The boys of the town were getting their pitching arms in great shape. It seemed a real pity that baseball season was about over.

I flopped on the bunk and tried to work up some brilliant scheme for escape. I couldn't. Though I have no doubt that Ben could have outlined three or four beauties right off the top of his head.

The only thing I seemed to have left was the hope I could convince someone he should listen to my side of it.

I gave that some downright serious thinking, and in the end the only thing that seemed to show any promise whatever was Marshal French's bent for letter-of-the-law actions. It seemed the only weak spot in the armor of pure hate he wore whenever he was around me. If you could call that a weakness.

The next time French set foot in his office I was waiting for him—well, where else would I be?—with my words picked out in advance.

"I have the right to an attorney," I shouted, loud and fast as I could.

French looked startled for just a moment before he started yelling, "Shut up, you lousy . . ." etc., etc., and so on. A very abusive youngster, Marshal French.

Thereafter for the rest of that day I would shut up and be good just long enough to hope he wasn't expecting it, then holler out my claim. "I have the right to an attorney."

And he would holler back.

Twice he got so mad he stomped out of the office, but I greeted him with it again when he came back. That night before his poker session he went through his punch-the-dummy routine.

He returned maybe three hours later, and I couldn't really understand the ugly expression he wore. There was a distinct bulge of coin in his pocket that he hadn't had when he left, so he should have been in a good mood.

He explained it himself. I yelled my "I have the right" piece to him and instead of blowing up mad he just looked meaner and unhappier. He stalked over to the cell door and took hold of the bars with white-knuckled fists.

"The . . . judge . . . says," he told me in his explain-to-the-idiot tone, "that . . . you . . . have . . . the . . . right . . . to . . . see . . . a . . . lawyer." He looked like he had a mouth full of bile and nowhere to spit. "Do . . . you . . . under . . . stand . . . me?"

There was no point in trying to antagonize him further. I nodded instead of speaking to him.

"He . . . will . . . be . . . here . . . in . . . the . . . morning."

I nodded again.

I wanted to laugh or to shout. Small as it was, it was a victory. And I don't figure to admit that I'm dead until I've been in the ground three days.

CHAPTER 14

The lawyer stood looking at me. He seemed to find me as distasteful as French did.

"Good morning," I said. "I thought you were going on an elk hunt."

Farley shrugged. "I am, but not until next week. This shouldn't take long."

"Oh." After all, what can you say to something like that? "And if it took longer?"

Again he shrugged. "The county is paying fifty dollars for your defense."

I rolled over on my bunk so I could lie on my stomach and watch him. "What would your normal fee be?"

"It would depend on the client's financial health. In your case . . . the county's fifty dollars, I suppose."

"And for a local businessman?"

He gave me a tight, snide smile. "You presume the impossible."

"At least you talk to me as if I were capable of understanding the language."

"Do I? I suppose I *am* somewhat confused. After our previous meeting, I mean."

"It would be awkward," I agreed, "making such an extreme adjustment."

"I'm sure I can manage it."

"You needn't be so eager. Anyway, humor me for the moment."

He looked puzzled. "About what?"

"Oh, good grief. About your fee."

"Oh yes. That again. Well . . . I suppose, in a case of such severity, perhaps two hundred. Maybe a little more if the details were, uh, sordid."

"Finc. Get the marshal to fetch my money belt from the safe and hand it to me."

"Whatever for? He counted the money, you know. Eleven dollars. All in bills." There was a trace of embarrassment in his expression. "It will be applied toward my fee, of course."

"Counselor. Please. You're humoring me, remember?"

He held up a hand. "All right."

He was back in a moment. He tossed the belt through the bars. I retrieved it from the floor and poked inside the long, narrow pouch. Farley took on a sickly look. "I hope you don't have a derringer hidden in there."

"Fine time to think of that, Counselor. But no, I don't have. Believe me, I would have except that I never anticipated being in such circumstances. Ah. Here it is." I plucked the slim fold of paper free and handed it to him through the bars. "It is a letter of credit. You have my authorization to draw three hundred dollars against it. I am sure the banker here will be delighted to handle it for you. If that will help convince you to be *my* lawyer instead of the county's, come back and we'll talk some more."

I went back to my bunk and lay with my face against the wall.

"But . . . But this is a substantial amount, Williams. Sixty-five thousand dollars. I mean . . ."

It was the first time he'd used my name since he arrived. Maybe we were getting somewhere after all.

But then I wondered. Farley's voice hardened again. "Where would some mule-riding drifter come by a document like this?"

I whirled from the bunk and confronted him through the steel barrier that separated us. I could not keep the anger and frustration from my voice. "Now listen to me, Counselor. Listen real close. Not once. Not once, mind you, has anyone in this town asked *me* anything. Anything at all. On any subject.

"No, not you fine people of Apishapa City. You listened to Mr. Benjamin Trask. You took a look at a homely, mule-riding stranger, and just that quick you had me catalogued neat as a butterfly on a specimen board, pins and all.

"Just like that, I was some low-life grub line drifter, prob'ly half-witted and most certainly perverted. A total disgrace to humanity." I shook my head.

"Did it never occur to you, Counselor, that I do not speak like your average, everyday half-wit? Did you not notice, Counselor, that when I arrived in your fair town I did not spend my time leering with evil intent at little girls in the schoolyard? That perhaps I had a reason for making myself presentable and asking questions of one of the community's better class of citizens?"

"No," I roared at him. "You did not, did you? None of that ever entered your mind, Counselor. After all, why allow facts to stand in the way of a nice, neat, ready-made conclusion? Why go through all the bother of independent thinking when Good Citizen Trask had already done it for you? Why . . . ? Ah, forget it. If you don't understand already, you never will." My spurt of anger had exhausted itself. And me. I do not believe I have ever felt lower, not even when I was lying alone with Ben's bullet through my back.

Farley faced me through the bars, but his eyes were cast down. He had been fidgeting with the letter of credit. Now he looked up, his eyes meeting mine. He thrust the paper back at me. "I'll collect my fee when the job is done," he said.

I nodded. "All right."

"And if you don't mind, I think I should come in. We, uh, need to sit and talk out quite a few things."

"All right."

I believe Farley surprised French with his request to enter my cell, but the marshal gave no more opposition than a wondering look. When Farley asked him to leave, he did so.

"Now then." Farley pointed to the paper still in my hand. "That. One assumes a fair degree of respectability in a man carrying that kind of financial authority. Now. Whom do you represent?"

"Myself, Counselor." His eyebrows shifted upward a notch. "Or perhaps I should say, my family. My mother—even the most heinous criminals have them, you know. My sisters. Their husbands and children.

"We raise beef, Counselor. Our family has run beeves on open range for the past fifty years. Open range is already a thing of the past. There are some die-hards in the Panhandle and a few more in the south country who refuse to see it. I think they are wrong. They have been forced off their old ranges and think they have found substitutes there. I guess there's some of the same thing up north of here.

"We are being forced from our old range, too. We can't buy it up. The best land goes for ten, even twenty dollars an acre. Brush land costs one to as much as two dollars. And brush cattle, our cattle, require huge amounts of land and a minimal tax rate." I quizzed Farley with my eyes and he nodded his comprehension.

"Right. So we are forced to move. We have sold our steers and most of our stock cows, range delivery. To another die-hard, of course. He thinks he's getting a bargain. We've tried to tell him otherwise, but . . ."

"I know the type."

"Yes. Anyway, I located some good range in Utah. Deeded land, not open. That letter of credit is for the purchase of a hundred fifty sections, fifty cents an acre. And some left over in case I like his stock cows. We won't attempt to ship all the range will carry."

Farley shook his head. "And for this you saddled a mule and took off riding?"

"Not exactly. I could have gone by rail and coach in a tenth the time, but . . . Frankly, I wanted a chance to just wander for a while."

I looked at my hands, those vaguely misshapen things at the end of simian arms. I looked back at Farley. "I thought it would be . . . enjoyable for a change. I never married. I suppose it is obvious why that is so. There was no real need for me at home right now. All the cattle had been transferred to the buyer's name except two thousand bred cows being held in fenced pasture. The hands and my brothers-in-law could handle them without me.

"It had been . . . I've been on that ranch or else following a herd of beef somewhere on behalf of the ranch every day of my life since my father died. That was when I was nineteen and . . . away from home.

"For a while there . . ." I could not help but laugh. "For a while there, I really felt good. Free. It was . . . fun . . . to just get on a horse and ramble around on my own."

"I see," Farley said.

For a time there was an awkward silence. Then Farley asked, curious for some reason I cannot fathom, "What were you doing when you were called home?"

"It doesn't matter now, of course."

"No."

Yet I found that I wanted to tell him. I had never discussed it with anyone before. Pointless. Maybe now I did because I might have little chance in the future to discuss anything with anyone. "I was at school," I said.

"Cadet. Virginia Military Institute. Third year. It was . . . a fine institution. My father had served with several VMI officers during the war. He thought highly of the school. And of them."

"Do you wish you had been able to make a career in the military, then?"

"Good heavens, no." I looked at him. "I must be sounding terribly maudlin. Steeped in self-pity. I never could have enjoyed military command. To begin with, leadership should be undertaken with the consent of those led if not by their selection. Certainly it should not be decided by Congressional decree. At least for me. I don't exactly have an inspiring appearance. No one should be forced to submit himself so absolutely to my authority. And anyway, I'm sorta independent-minded myself. I wouldn't want to spend my life taking orders any more than giving them.

"No, Counselor, what I enjoyed there was the education. The intricacies of maneuver. The study of tactics. And at the same time exposure to the classical studies, to protocol, to geology and yet without having to stuff ourselves away in some dark corner. Plenty of activity. Saber drill. Rifle drill. Marksmanship. Mounted games." I laughed. "It was all quite a lark, really."

"What would you have done had you completed your studies?"

"Why, I'd have come home, of course. There was work to be

done. And don't get me wrong. There is nothing I could imagine that I would enjoy more than what I have been doing. I suppose . . . I suppose that all I might have changed would have been the last year and a half of study. There was so much I still wanted to learn. And I never will know how much I've been able to find on my own or how much I missed. I think that's what galls me so bad. I don't know what I missed learning."

I stopped short of a sudden. "Do you know something? I just told you that that galls me. And . . . it's the truth. It does, in a way. I never thought about that before. But I guess it's so."

I got up and stomped around in the tiny circle the cell allowed. "Isn't it strange that I never saw that?"

Farley took his time about pulling a cigar from inside his coat, clipping the twist, and forming a coal. When he was satisfied with the thick puffs of blue smoke it produced, he said, "I don't find it surprising at all, Williams. Not if a man finds self-pity distasteful." He pulled at the cigar until he was wreathed in the pungent smoke. "And I suppose as a youngster you might have mistaken self-honesty for self-pity. Possible?"

"Ye-e-e-ss. Yes, I suppose it might have been."

"Ah, but then again, criminal perverts are not likely to be honest either with themselves or with others."

I was taken aback completely. My eyes leapt toward him. But there was no contemptuous sneer. Instead there was a small upward turn at the corners of his mouth.

"I didn't mean to startle you. Poor taste, of course, but a jest nonetheless."

"Whew." I sat heavily onto the bunk beside him.

"And now, Mr. Williams, I believe I should leave off being a confessor in the priestly sense and return to my workaday calling. I want you to tell me, exactly and completely and with the utmost honesty, everything you know about Janet Trask, her brothers, her conduct, their conduct, your own conduct. Everything." He sat back and drew on his cigar again until the coal turned a sputtering red.

"All right, Counselor. To begin with the girl's name is Cates, not Trask. And she's no more of a lunatic than I am. No. Let me rephrase that. Just say, she is not a lunatic. The first I saw of her was about two weeks ago, and . . ."

It was a long enough story, but Farley gave full attention to every word and did not even interrupt to request clarification. I mentally crossed my fingers when I came to the part about Leo. I'd killed him. And if I misjudged Louis Farley, he could use my own words to ensure that I be hanged by the neck until dead.

But then, what other choice did I have? I plunged ahead, leaving out no detail that I could dredge from memory.

CHAPTER 15

The next day—a Tuesday it was, though I hadn't been keeping track of late—Farley came by late in the afternoon. He was dust-caked and hadn't shaved, and I must say he looked altogether more human and approachable that way. Maybe it was only that I was more used to dealing with men who smelled of horse sweat, but I found myself feeling some easier about him. I'd had some real uneasy feelings when he hadn't come by earlier in the day.

He had himself let inside the cell, and Marshal French left the office without waiting to be asked.

The marshal had not been a happy man that day either. I believe he was afraid I would pull something mean and underhanded on him. Like maybe turning out to be not the wandering half-wit he'd been treating me as.

Farley sat on my bunk and went through his cigar preparation routine. His attention still seemed to be wholly on the glowing cigar when he spoke. "I got to doubting you yesterday morning." He paused, plainly expecting me to say something, but I did not.

"I decided to sit down with Dave French and Ben Trask and go over all you'd told me."

My blood begun to run cold, but there was nothing I could say or do now to change anything.

Farley went on. "I was sure it was the right thing to do. I would have. I was about to. But I couldn't find Trask, nor his brother either. I had dinner and thought about it." He looked at me. "Your story really sounds preposterous, you know."

I nodded.

"Anyway, I didn't do it. The truth is that I got to thinking about that letter of credit. It doesn't speak too well of me to admit it, but I guess that did influence me some. Got me to *wanting* to believe you, if you know what I mean."

Well, it was jolly well supposed to. That was the reason I'd showed it to the man after picking up on his interest in money when we talked before. What I hadn't expected from him was this much honesty.

"So what I did instead," he said, "was ride out to where you said this fight took place."

"You know the spot that well?" It surprised me. He'd seemed strictly a town type of person. I guess I had underestimated him on several counts.

Farley grinned. "I got my first desert sheep near that seep you told me about. I've hunted the area twice since."

"You hunt meat or heads?"

"Meat first, but that's no trouble. Then special heads. Anything outsized or genuinely unusual. Why?"

It was my turn to grin. And I was starting to like this fellow, though I hadn't expected to. "Down on our old range in the brush country we got a strain of whitetail that aren't real much for size in the body but for some reason they grow big, twisty racks that look like some kind of thorn tree. The old fellers will go twenty points or better. You might want to put one on your wall before my family moves to Utah."

"You're trying to give me a good reason to get you out of here?"

"Uh huh."

"I've had worse fees, and a lot worse reason for doing something."

"Good. But, uh . . . what did you find on your trip? Anything that will help?"

"Not a thing that would help before a jury. But enough to make me believe you, maybe."

I waited for him to continue. "You said you'd dropped a bacon rind, but there was no sign of it." I started to speak, but he held up his hand impatiently. "I know. It's been over a week. It is a long time eaten and gone by now. What I found was something you hadn't told me about. From that jut of rock right clean down the side of the slope there is a long, clear scrape. Plain as a chalk mark on the stone. Probably put there by your belt buckle."

"I never noticed it."

"Can't say that's surprising considering the shape you must have been in." He shuddered. "I wouldn't want to take that drop. Not in the best condition I ever will be in, much less with two bullets through me."

"It seemed a pretty good idea at the time."

"It worked. And . . . well, I guess I believe you. That's all."

"What about Leo? Did you find a grave?"

"I didn't go up to search. It was coming dark, and I didn't want to make the climb in the dark or take time to look for a way to ride up. I started back before dawn this morning."

"All right. Now what do we do?"

"I can tell you what we *don't* do. We don't try to take your story to a jury. You were absolutely right to think that testimony about you and the girl using the same assumed name would be dangerous. I dare say it would be fatal."

"Is that what I'm looking at here? Hanging?"

"That would be the maximum penalty under law, yes. And as a matter of practicality, I would expect it."

"I was sort of assuming so, but . . . no one had made it official before."

"A conviction would ruin your whole day."

"Well said, Counselor. So what do we do?"

"I can't see any way to win your case in trial proceedings. What we have to do is head it off before we go that far."

"I thought the question was when I go to trial, not if."

"Oh no." Farley shook his head vigorously. "Before a trial you must be indicted by a grand jury. And before THAT can happen, a formal charge must be filed. Which hasn't been done either."

"What? If I'm not charged with any crime, what in the billy blue blazes am I doing in this jail cell?"

Farley's smile was tight and smug. "Let's not go around mentioning that, shall we? Everyone thinks of you as someone who needs hanging, and they feel the job is as good as done. The next circuit court session won't meet for seven weeks, and they won't convene the grand jury until about two weeks before it. The information needn't be filed until then if French doesn't bother before."

"In the meantime I just sit here?"

"In the meantime we try to find some good reason why the marshal—meaning French AND the good, leading citizens of the town—should change their minds about your probable guilt as a perverted degenerate."

"And I sit here?"

"And you sit here. Quietly. Not complaining. Not talking with anyone but me."

"Could you at least get the marshal to quit thumping on me? I'm getting a bit impatient with the man. Much more of it and I'm going to have to see if I can't wedge his head between his bars."

Farley gave me a slap on the knee. "I think we can straighten that out, Williams. And don't worry more than you have to. You've made one convert anyway." He stood. "I'm going to go read a little law now and maybe stop by the courthouse annex for some inspiration."

"They offer it bottled these days?"

"And bonded, sir. And bonded." He gave me a broad, friendly smile and went to the door to yell for French to come open up.

I could not help wishing I had the same privilege.

Farley developed a habit of dropping in on me. Interviewing the client, he termed it. Actually there was little enough to discuss along that line.

Neither of us had any good ideas about how we could convince anyone that I was an innocent victim of a Ben Trask plot. Nor very darn many poor ideas.

So for the most part we sat and chatted. And sipped at a lovingly filled flask Farley kept in his coat pocket. And occupied ourselves with an amusement which, we discovered with considerable delight, was of mutual interest. Chess.

Farley was positively addicted to the game, and I confess to having an inordinate passion for it myself.

It had seemed most odd to discover, but rarely has our roster of working cowhands not included at least one other person who also plays. There is a separate compartment in our roundup wagon where a board and pieces may always be found. Many's the night I have spent playing by lantern light with the sound of singing night herders for a musical backdrop. Yet in contrast, Farley told me it was almost impossible for him to find an opponent in Apishapa City.

Perhaps his lack of practice had something to do with my run of good fortune in our combat. And in truth his game sharpened as he learned my style of play—primarily one of continual attack with knight and bishop spearheads and close pawn support. It became increasingly difficult to entrap him, and I believe both of us enjoyed our play the more for it.

Before a week had passed Farley had quit carrying a folded board under his arm when he came to the jail. Instead he installed a small table in my cell with the board squares inlaid into the surface with contrasting wood tones. He also brought for himself a comfortably padded chair. This I appreciated even—maybe especially—when he was not there to use it.

We were seated on opposite sides of the table on a Wednesday afternoon the week following our first client-lawyer meeting, Farley in his chair and I perched on the side rail of my bunk. Farley had drawn white for the game and was trying to use his king's knight to disrupt my habitual screen of forward pawns. I reached absently for the flask, on the table beside the inlaid board, while I studied the pieces.

"Hidee, Stumpy," a cheerful voice called from the cell door. I looked up, my concentration abruptly ended. A tiny man stood there, wizened and bowlegged. The ends of his mustaches drooped well below the corners of his mouth, and he had sharp features coming together in a weasel-like point in the center of his face over a practically chinless jaw. Despite the heat he wore bullhide leggins—chaps, they call them up north—a calfskin vest and an old and much-worn coat. His hatbrim was bent almost vertical over the ears and was creased into a sharp point at the front.

As far as I could tell from one spring to the next, he had been wearing the same outfit for the past ten years.

"Hey, Ned. Didn't expect to see you this time o' year."

Farley had swiveled around in his chair, so I stood and gestured toward the aging man. "This here's Ned Roberts," I said. "Oldest living bronc buster in captivity. He comes by our place every April to take the kinks out of our rough string before roundup. He works cheap. Onliest reason we hire him."

Ned grinned, exposing yellow stubs that used to be teeth. "That's the truth."

"This here is Louis Farley, Ned. He's standing up as my lawyer."

"Pleased to meetcha," Ned said, and Farley nodded. "I heerd you needed sumpin like that," Ned told me. "Fella said you wuz takin' up with little girls these days or sumpin like that. I can understand it. Man as ugly as you. No other way for you, I'd say."

"I got only one consolation," I said. "At least I ain't both ugly an' old too." I went to the door and pumped Ned's hand. "Just passin' through town?"

"Uh-huh. I got a daughter up to Colorado Springs. I winter with her these days. Tryin' to break myself in to uselessness gradual-like."

"Yeah, another year or so an' you'll be too old to ride a stick horse without getting throwed."

Farley joined us. He had a smile on his face and seemed to of caught the drift of things all right. He stuck his hand through the bars to shake with Ned. "You must be a fine rider, Mr. Roberts."

"Now you're a man that knows quality, lawyer." Farley bowed toward him with a small, quick motion, scarce more than a slight inclination of his head and upper body.

"Say, Ned, what's the chance you could come by our place early next year? Say by about a month," I asked him.

"I reckon it could be done. Are the Williamses up to something special?"

"I thought you'd of heard. We're moving to Utah. We'll take a herd of stock cows and most of our broodmares. Everything else has been sold."

"Sure, I'll be there to put your horses in shape." Ned stroked his chin. "Moving onto deeded range, are ya?"

"Yeah."

"Well, you been talkin' about it long enough. I'm just surprised yore mama gave in."

"She's stubborn, Ned. Not stupid."

"That's fer sure. A lotta woman, your mama. Like they say. Salt o' the earth. An' yore daddy too."

"It sounds like you know the family well," Farley said.

"I'd say I know 'em. I broke horses for the Willumses when Stumpy here was still wearin' dresses, an' when I come back south from the Oregon country—after his daddy Lowell was taken, that was—I went back to 'em and been takin' the kinks out for them ever since. So soft ones like this boy can do the easy part." Ned seemed right proud of himself, and I was just as proud of him. What he'd said wouldn't hurt me a bit with Farley.

The lawyer smiled at us and politely returned to the chess table.

Ned pushed his face against the bars and beckoned me close with a crooked finger. In a rasping and none too quiet whisper he told me, "I'll be around town, Stumpy. No need to go up to my girl's place yet awhile. She ain't expecting me any special month. What I thought was, any time you want, you hang your shirt over the cell window like you was gonna dry it out. If you do that I'll be watchin', an' the nex' morning I'll see can we persuade the lawman to turn you outta here. Or I can do it tonight if you want."

I smiled at him. "I hope it won't come to that. But . . . you're a right good friend, Ned." I think it embarrassed him, for his face colored a shade darker than the wind had already burned it.

"Do you want I should send a tellygram to your sisters' menfolk?" he asked in his croaking whisper.

I grimaced. "It wouldn't do no more good than to stir up the women an' make them fretful. And the boys couldn't do anything."

"Yeah," he said, "I reckon you know best. They ain't too awful bad fellas, though. But you handle it however you want."

Ned turned to go but then shoved his face close to the bars

again. "Mister lawyer," he said, "this here's a pretty good ol' boy. You do right by him, hear?"

"I intend to," Farley said.

When Ned had gone I returned to my side of the table and moved my queen bishop.

Farley studied the pieces. "You have some good friends," he said, still looking at them.

"I've been fortunate that way."

"Mind you, I did not intentionally eavesdrop," he said.

"It would have been hard not to hear," I agreed.

"As an officer of the court . . ."

"I know," I said quickly, cutting off what he would have had to say. "Don't worry."

He looked up with a smile. "I notice you did not say you would not do it. Just that I should not worry about it."

I shrugged. "You heard an offer but no acceptance. Surely you wouldn't want to get old Ned in trouble just for his kindness."

"No. Of course not." He used his pawn for a capture, and the game was properly launched. I felt the tenseness of anticipation as I leaned forward to move my bishop.

CHAPTER 16

Farley was grinning broadly when he came in, and I got a strong impression he could hardly wait for the marshal to leave after locking him in with me.

"My telegrams came back," he said excitedly as soon as French was through the street door.

"What telegrams?" It was news to me. "It's too dang early for a pardon from the governor."

Farley waved a sheaf of Western Union message forms under my nose. "These telegrams, and they might be almost as good as a note from our leader. I, uh, got the germ of an idea when your friend Roberts was here the other day. Ned and I got together for a long talk that evening. And I think it may have paid off."

"Grand. Wonderful. I'm ecstatic. What are you talking about?" But I *was* starting to get excited. Whatever Farley had was catching.

"Look here, Williams. How did you win me over?"

"I let you beat me at chess yesterday."

"And it helped, believe me. But really now. Respectability. That was it in a nutshell. Respectability. As a tramp we'd expect a pack of lies from you, so why bother asking any questions? As a man of good family, honored by friends, head of a sizable ranch operation, good school background and—most important—of impeccable financial status . . . well . . . to a man like that, one listens."

"That isn't right, Lou." We had gotten along well enough for me to be calling him that now. "I'm no more guilty now than I was before I flashed that bank letter at you."

"Of course it isn't right. Never said it was, did I? But it *is* a fact of life, and we'll put it to advantage if we can. Or do you stand so staunchly on high principle that we throw away the only ammunition we have?"

"Not hardly, Counselor. Not. Hardly."

"So." Farley was brisk again. "So maybe we can use these to divert some more local thinking into new channels." He riffled the stack of papers with his thumbnail. "These, sir, are telegrams. From . . ." He consulted a list drawn from an inside coat pocket. "From Ronald Gordon, sheriff, McMullen County, Texas. The Honorable Cletus A. Tyson, representative, Congress of the United States, from San Antonio, Texas. The Honorable P. G. Woodside, circuit judge, Laredo, Texas. Philo F. Franklin, president of the Stockman's Bank of Commerce, Tilden, Texas. William L. Shields, president, Bank of San Antonio, Texas. L. F. B. Pearce, president, South Texas Stockman's Association, Beeville, Texas. 'Jube' Watson, brands inspector, McMullen County, Texas. And so on, and so on and so forth."

"Where in the world did you . . . ?"

Farley stopped me with an upheld hand and a smug look. "Some of the list came from Roberts. Some went out by title and came back with signatures." He smiled. "It wasn't difficult really, once we got the idea. I must say we rather enjoyed it. Of course we ran up an unconscionable bill with Western Union. It will be added to your bill as expenses, itemized of course."

"Of course. And what do they say?"

"My personal favorite is from Sheriff Gordon. You know him, I believe?"

"I do," I said with a chuckle, "and Western Union would never transmit whatever he said. Not in his own words, anyway. They'd have to clean it up first."

"Perhaps so. At any rate, here is the text of his message, as received by the telegrapher here. 'HONORABLE SIRS STOP KNOW SUBJECT IN CUSTODY YOUR CITY STOP IF STUMPY SAYS SUN WILL RISE TOMORROW IN WEST COMMA STRONGLY RECOMMEND YOU CLOSE BLINDS THAT SIDE HOUSE BEFORE RETIRING COLON SUN WILL SO RISE STOP.' And an official signature."

I grinned. "Sounds more like Benjie Zakkut's wording but maybe Uncle Ron's sentiments."

"Uncle Ron?"

"About the same relationship you have to Uncle Zeke or Zack or whatever your judge's name is here."

"Oh yes. Uncle Orville. I can understand that all right."

"And the other messages?"

"Different wording. Same story. I would say you have some very good friends back home."

"Better than I ever realized, I'll tell you that." I sat on my bunk and toyed with a white rook absent-mindedly. "Do you really think those telegrams should help?"

"Do I? Do I ever. Listen, Stumpy, with these to shove under the noses of a few selected friends and colleagues here in town, there is going to be some rapid rethinking. All of a sudden people are going to start remembering that the Trask boys are just as much strangers here as you are. And all we really know about them is what they told us themselves. As for you . . ." He slapped the stack of telegrams. "You are now the respectable Mr. Williams of Tilden, Texas. Cattleman and demonstrably upright citizen. My friend, I think we are in business."

I don't know what all Farley told his select group of fellow citizens. For obvious reasons I was not present at the several discussions they must have had. And of course not all of them believed what he told them. Not all were willing to change their minds.

But there were enough.

On Monday morning, early enough that the alley outside my cell window was still in full shadow, Farley and Marshal Dave French entered the little brick jailhouse together. I could tell from Louis' expression that he had good news.

French threw the lever that allowed my cell door to open. He swung wide the heavy, steel-barred closure and let it stand open. Farley made no move to enter.

With beaming satisfaction Louis slapped a paper into my hand. "End of the chess games," he said.

I looked at the flimsy slip of white. "Fee for services," it read, "$50.00. Expenses, telegrams, $27.80. Total owed, $77.80."

"There is also this," he said, and gave me another bit of paper.

It had an engraved letterhead. Apishapa City Hotel. It was written with a flourishing, almost ornate hand.

"Sirs. It is with extreme regret that we must leave on urgent, unexpected business. My brother Thos. McP. Trask or self shall return if at all possible to testify at the trial of the criminal Williams. Thank you for many kindnesses, Etc." It was signed with a B. Trask so fancily scrawled as to be almost illegible.

"I take it that my friends have decamped?"

"Into the sunset," Louis said gleefully.

"Why?"

"Oh, maybe it was because several of their closer supporters had been invited into our discussions, once it was obvious which way things were shifting."

"Very neat, Counselor. Very neat indeed."

"In the absence of a complaining witness, I have no choice but to release you," French said. He did not seem overjoyed to have me on the loose again.

As for myself, it is hard to say what I felt. One would expect jubilation, gratitude, laughter, a desire for celebration. I felt none of them. More a numbness. And a dim, remote flicker of contained anger. But jubilation? No.

I stepped across the threshold of the cell—no longer *my* cell, but *the* cell—and stood waiting, looking at French. He seemed puzzled at first, then quickly gathered together my money belt, boots, gun, and other personal possessions. I put them on, stowed appropriate items in the pockets dictated by long habit, and waited, still staring at the marshal.

"Your mule and other things are at the livery. Jordan's. South end of town."

"The city will pay the fees, of course," Louis said. It was not a question, and French gave no reaction. He stood nervously returning my gaze.

"No apologies, Marshal?"

His face reddened, in anger not in shame, I thought, and he began to bluster. "Man has a job to do . . ." he was saying. Something about "good faith" and "just following orders" and more.

I looked at Farley and hiked my eyebrows. "Dave here would

be one to file a battery charge at the very least, Stumpy," he said over the sound of French's continuing voice.

I pushed down the desire I felt to plant a hard right across the marshal's face. With Farley beside me and French still talking behind us in rising and now strident tones, I left the building.

The sun outdoors was bright. I had to squint against the glare, but I did not mind at all. Here outside the confines of that jailhouse alley the air carried the scent of growing things and had the damp freshness of having passed over cool, shaded ground. I did not realize until that moment just how much I'd missed that. I filled my lungs with air so sweet I could taste it, the same taste as is given by a rushing stream of new-melted snow.

I stretched my shoulder muscles beneath my coat and made a face.

"Something wrong?" Lou asked.

"These clothes. I think they've grown to me. Smell like a dead hide, anyhow. And to think they were brand new when I walked in that door."

His answering grin, I believe, was doubly appreciative. I could not have been real pleasant to be next to. "Where now?" he asked.

"There's so much I need to do that I don't know what should come first," I told him. "Is there a good restaurant at the hotel?" He nodded. "Then let's say I meet you there in an hour. I need to stop at the bank and the haberdasher's and then straight to the barbershop for a hot bath and a shave. Then I want to stand you to the best meal this town can put together."

"Done," he said. "And with that much warning, how about if I have them lay on some Rocky Mountain oysters, roast duck in wine sauce, ice cream with sliced peaches, and a quart of decent brandy."

"Done and done, Counselor. You do know how to treat a jail-bird."

"An ex-jailbird, sir. Thanks to expert legal defense."

My step was light as I headed for the bank.

CHAPTER 17

Red-faced railroad men with red scarves at their throats and limp, blue-striped caps worn like badges of office muscled the ramp into place to unload my mule and a dun mare from an otherwise empty cattle car. There was a smell of burnt coal in the air and a crunch of brittle cinders underfoot with every step. The noises of a rail yard have always been faintly offensive to me. Too much of it, I believe. The hiss and rattle of steam. Crash of metal couplings and squeal of brakes. Baggage cart wheels clattering. Chug and lurch of engines driving. And, littered among all the rest, the sound of men shouting in attempts to make themselves heard.

A thin blond youth wearing the scarf but no cap led the mule down the planking. Gray came readily enough, setting his feet judiciously but not pulling back on the rope even though his long ears were laid flat in annoyance or possibly discomfort. Behind him a shorter, stockier youngster led the mare. She stopped, trembling, at the car door, then launched herself in a leg-churning scramble for the safety of solid ground. The boy holding the rope was jerked forward with her but managed to keep his hold on the lead. He looked as if he would have been much more comfortable with a linchpin than with a lead rope.

Having just had an excellent lesson in such things, I remembered to think of appearances for a change and tossed a coin to a small boy perched on a barrel by the depot platform. He was delighted to lead the mule behind me when I walked into the town proper a hundred yards away.

When the mule was safely established in a livery I went looking for the grandest hotel in Pueblo and found it, appropriately enough, in the Grande, a block away from the courthouse.

A slick-haired clerk with a pinched and unhappy face assigned me a room on the second floor. "No guns worn in the city," he said primly. "Local ordinance." I guess my studiously respectable clothes did not make a great deal of difference after all. I knew no amount of cloth could make me handsome, but I'd at least hoped to look presentable. Not like some ape dressed in party clothes.

But there I was feeling sorry for myself again like a schoolgirl with two whole dances vacant on my card. I should have been feeling pretty good, and well I knew it. I shoved such thoughts aside and set my just-off-the-shelf valise on the massive dressing table in my room.

The room was comfortable enough. A huge, soft bed with a post at each corner of the head and footboards taller than me. A pair of needle-point-covered chairs flanking a round tea table, and a wide wardrobe next to windows that looked out over the street. A small shaving stand and mirror were tucked into a corner.

In deference to local law I removed my gunbelt and hung it inside the wardrobe. But in the interest of self-preservation I took the old Remington from its holster and tucked it into my waistband where I hoped it would remain hidden beneath my coat.

I fingered my jaw and decided the shave could wait a few hours more. Then I headed for the courthouse.

The court clerk was a tanned and healthy-looking fellow in his twenties somewhere, and he seemed to have his sights set on a long and rewarding career at the public trough. He was courteous and helpful without being subservient. He also seemed quite competent. When I told him what I wanted he had a ready smile and a quick answer.

"Yes, sir. That would be in OR Book 4, page . . . oh . . . about in the seventies. Judgment entered sometime in June, I believe. I'll have it for you in a moment, sir," he said cheerfully. His smile was engaging, and he would have been a handsome boy if he'd had a bit more jaw. He was quite likeable.

"Do you remember all of the court actions so well?"

"Not quite, sir, but most of them, I would say. There are not so very many. And if this is the one I am thinking of, I've looked it up before. Telegraph request for confirmation of the judgment, it was, sir. Excuse me for just a moment, please."

He was back in no time with a heavy, linen-bound volume that he opened wide on the counter between us, paged through briefly, and then spun on the counter for me to examine. "Would that be the correct action, sir?"

"Yes, thank you. You've been very kind."

He smiled and inclined his head and turned discreetly away to busy himself at a desk on the far side of the room.

It was indeed the document I wanted. An order signed by Judge Hubert E. Hinsley, declaring Mistress Janet Cates a mental incompetent. The judge apparently was not one for false modesty. In the decree he lauded his own magnanimity in refraining from committing the legal nonperson to the Colorado Home for the Feeble Minded. Instead he assigned guardianship of the girl to an adult blood relative identified as one Joshua Davis. No doubt that was the oft-mentioned uncle, presumably on the Trask side of the family.

I noticed that in this official record book of the court Miss Janet's surname was listed as Cates. And while I hadn't seen the message myself, I was almost certain that the marshal back in Apishapa City, and later Louis Farley as well, had told me about a telegram confirming the incompetence of Janet Cates Trask. A minor but interesting variation there.

No address was given in the court document for Josh Davis. Well, that was all right. If the Trask boys had enough power around Pueblo to get a court order from a tame judge and to monkey with the wording of telegraph messages, they pretty much had to be from around here somewhere close. Maybe right in town. That thought made me more glad than ever of the old Remington under my coat.

I nodded my thanks to the court clerk and beckoned him to return to the counter that separated public from employee.

"That was just what I wanted to see," I told him. "Would you happen to know where I could reach the man named here? It's, uh, Joshua Davis," I said, running a finger down the page until I came to the appropriate section.

"No, I surely don't, sir. Sorry."

"I wonder if the judge might know."

His eyes flicked toward the signature. "That was Judge Hinsley, wasn't it?" There was a ghost of a smile on his lips. Or a hint of scorn. It could have been either. "I really don't think the judge could tell you either, sir."

"No? Why?"

"Let me put it this way, sir. I don't believe the judge *would* tell you. I remember he was quite upset when he heard about the earlier inquiry, by telegraph. The judge is very . . . shall I say . . . concerned . . ."

"Defensive?" I injected.

The clerk smiled. "Let's stick with concerned, sir. About his court rulings. Very proud man, His Honor."

"But a fair and honorable man," I said with an implied question mark in the tone of voice. "An honorable and upright jurist. Credit to the bench and all that."

"But of course, sir. Elected when Colorado became a state and re-elected continuously since then."

"Perhaps I understand."

"Perhaps you do, sir," he said. His lips were still drawn upward but now were held tighter across his teeth. I thought it a pity that this man would never speak too freely with a stranger. I thanked him and left.

For a time I idled around the city. I stopped in at a barbershop for a shave and boot blackening. Drank a cooling soda at an ice-cream parlor. Browsed through a stationer's shop and selected a box of decorated note paper that the shopkeeper mailed off to Mother for me. In none of them was anyone familiar with Joshua Davis. I stopped back by the livery to satisfy myself that the mule was being tended properly. The beast was interested in a full hay net and took no notice of my visit.

During all of this time I kept a wary eye out for either of the Trask boys. In Apishapa City they had seen me first. I did not want it to happen again.

No one locally, at least no one I had yet asked, seemed to know where I could find Josh Davis, but not all paths were blocked by that. I went back to the courthouse.

The clerk was still at his desk. When I entered he had the quick smile turned on before he even looked to see who'd come in. It quivered a little and seemed ready to be withdrawn when he saw who I was.

"Yes, sir?"

"There is one more thing you might tell me if you would, please."

"Would it be about Judge Hinsley, sir?"

"It would not." He relaxed visibly. "It's a minor thing, is all. The telegraphed inquiry earlier."

"Yes?"

"You responded by telegram, I would assume."

"Yes."

"Who was it who sent the response?"

"I did, sir."

"No, I mean the telegrapher. Who transmitted it?"

"Oh, that would be Harry Broll. Night man at the Western Union office. It's at the railroad depot if you wanted to ask him something. I dropped the message off after work that evening."

"I shouldn't think I would need to bother Mr. Broll," I said. "You wouldn't happen to have a copy of the message by any chance, would you?"

The smile was firmly back in place now. "I certainly would. It's right here in the correspondence file." He leapt to a bank of wooden cabinets with deep drawers. Within moments he showed me a copy of the message. Janet Cates, it said. Not Trask.

Not that it proved anything. Anyone who'd alter a message about a public record would not be likely to leave proof of it lying about. All this did was show that the change had not been an innocent error of transcription here in the clerk's office. I thanked him again and left.

For some reason I never had the slightest suspicion that the clerk might have made the change when he gave the message to the telegraph operator. I suppose the reason is that the clerk seemed so chary of interpretations or actions that could jeopardize an ambitious political career that I never could have envisioned him as a party to a scheme not politically motivated. He simply struck me very strongly as someone who was so strongly oriented toward politics as a means to power that mere money would not be a strong inducement for him. While the Trasks seemed equally devoted toward money as a power tool. And those are NOT two sides of the same coin. One type seldom holds any brief for the other, one finding the other quite beyond his comprehension and therefore beneath his contempt.

It was still too early to be sure of finding Broll at work so I returned to the Grande for a rest and, later, an excellent meal. If I had spent most of my time in extreme discomfort since meeting Miss Janet, I was certainly making up for it now. I had never treated myself so well before, not even at the Stockman Association conventions, and I felt a little guilty about how much of the family's money I was spending. My dinner cost three dollars and fifty cents alone. I tried to justify it by telling myself I was putting up a front of respectability. The truth is that I was really sort of enjoying it for a change.

Broll was alone in an office dimly illuminated by a pair of oil lamps. They threw a field of yellow light across his desk with the telegraph key affixed to one corner like a shiny brass spider. That is another of the many modern instruments I will never understand. I do not know how it works, and its staccato clacking is but so much noise to my ears.

The telegrapher's face was in deep shadow when I entered. Only his hands and forearms and the front of his vest were illuminated. The hands were pale, the fingers long and exceptionally slender, tapering to points much more noticeable than my own. The nails, too, were unusually long, carefully rounded and meticulously clean. Hands like that must have been actively tended, almost on a daily basis. I had never seen such hands on a man, yet there was no question that was what he was. His wrists and what I could see of his arms beneath turned-back sleeve cuffs were well muscled and densely haired.

When he heard me come in he reached first to turn up the wicks of the lamps, then to the desk where lay a pad of paper and a rank of sharpened pencils. The lamps gave off a little more light.

Broll had a thin face, sallow and with cheeks sunken under high, prominent cheekbones. The skin was exceptionally smooth, flawless as a girl's.

For some reason I took an instant and intense dislike to him. Perhaps it was due to an accumulation of past frustration and recent pain. Certainly he was not responsible for any of the discomfort I had suffered at the hands of Ben and Tom Trask or of their late brother.

Broll looked at me expectantly, pencil in hand. It was plain no one had warned him to beware of anyone meeting my description.

I had been thinking about bribing the telegrapher into telling me what I wanted to know, but now, facing him, a wave of anger surged through me.

"Benjamin Trask," I said in a voice that fell harsh even on my own ears, like a snarl more than intelligent speech. "You altered a wire for him." It was not a question.

The color drained from Broll's face. In no more time than it took for him to hear the name spoken, he looked like a sick man, older and somehow shrunken. He shook his head weakly.

My right hand, hardened and scarred by rope and shovel and hot irons, clenched into a fist. I held it above him like a club and he shrank away from me, still shaking his head.

"You altered that wire, mister. You changed that one word. A girl could die because of that."

Broll's eyes were fixed, staring up at my fist. I fought back an impulse to smash my hand across his face. Trembling from the strain of holding back, I pointed an accusing finger under his nose.

"I didn't know," he whispered.

Broll shuddered. He licked dry lips and stared at my hand. "I didn't have any choice," he said. "Trask knows what it is I got to hide. I didn't have a choice."

"I don't care *why* you did it, mister. I don't want anything to do with the greed and the sicknesses Trask finds in people. I just want to find Trask."

Again Broll shook his head but more forcefully. The color was beginning to return to his features.

"I don't know where you'd find him. He comes sometimes. He goes. I don't know more than that." The words tumbled out. The relief he felt was plain to see.

Trask. The name itself was beginning to disgust me. He preyed upon people like a coyote cruising at the edge of a herd or a flock, waiting to find and to devour the weakest or the sickest of the bunch, fighting when he had to and then doing it viciously, without thought for anyone or anything but his own wants and his own needs.

"Joshua Davis, then. Where is he?"

Broll looked genuinely puzzled. "I never heard of this Davis," he said.

"Listen to me, Broll," I said, and my voice was tight and strained again. "You are going to tell me about Trask."

He had begun to relax but now, again, he cringed back in the swivel chair. The springs of the desk chair creaked, the sound overloud in the nearly dark room.

"I don't *know*." His voice was plaintive, pleading. "East. Somewhere east of here. I think that is the direction Trask comes from. I never asked. I don't want to know."

"When does he come? What time of day?"

"Afternoon, I think. Afternoon or evening. I don't know any more than that. I swear I don't."

"Ah-h-h!" I batted futilely at empty air. The anger and the irritation and the disgust I had been feeling drained away. This unfortunate creature could tell me nothing except that he was another of Trask's victims. I turned to leave.

Behind me I could hear the chair creak again.

"Mister," Broll said. I turned to look at him. There was a quiet, deep-running despair in his eyes. "Mister, I'm truly sorry."

"Yeah."

I went back to the Grande, knowing so little more than I had before. Still knowing nothing about where to find Benjamin Trask. Or Janet Cates. Somewhere she was alone with her enemies, and I did not know where. My thoughts that night were not good ones.

CHAPTER 18

I spent the next day wandering around the town. I accomplished nothing that way but to entertain myself. Still, before I left the town I wanted to speak with the Honorable Hubert E. Hinsley, circuit judge for Pueblo County. And I did not especially want to do it at the courthouse, nor during normal working hours.

In an office, surrounded by reminders of the power and dignity of his office, the judge might be harder to confront than at home where he would be amid whatever doubts and miseries assailed his private life. So I marked time.

On an impulse I went to the local newspaper and spent several hours leafing through back issues of their and other Colorado newspapers. It was a waste of time. And the editor was a fluttering, busy man who responded to questions as interruptions and irritations.

I waited until evening and then went to call on the judge.

The Hinsley home was a tall, narrow structure on a tiny lot, crowded in among other houses with no more to separate them than cinder-covered walkways barely wide enough to allow a coal cart through. The house was built well enough, with horizontal lap siding rather than the more common clapboard. At first glance it looked right tidy, but then one could notice the paint beginning to darken and flake up under the eaves. The houses nearby looked some better.

I let myself in through a peeling gate in the low picket fence. The gate spring creaked loud in the stillness of early evening.

A plump woman with strands of gray hair escaping from a loose bun came to the door before I ever reached it. She had her sleeves folded back and was wiping work- and water-reddened hands on a dish towel. I never did decide if she was the judge's missus or if she was just a housekeeper.

When I asked for the judge she led me to a study to the left of the center hall and went toward the back of the house without a murmur nor a peep. Quiet sort of person, she seemed.

The doors to the study were pulled closed save for a crack in the middle, so I knocked. It was a deep, rich voice that told me to come, a voice that would have went well for Fourth-of-July picnics or first game of the season barbecues.

Judge Hinsley was well on in age, running to fat and drooping jowls. Between the meat on his cheeks and the amount of side-burns he cultivated there, he looked like he'd been dewlapped on either side of his face. He was sprawled or maybe had been deposited in a big, leather-covered armchair near a fireplace so full of ash the stuff was spilling out onto the hearth. He had his coat off and his vest undone, and the cloth of his shirt gapped open between buttons from trying to contain so much belly. He had his feet propped on a leather stool. The shoes could have used new soles, and his stockings had a grimy, long-unwashed look about them. The stockings were bunched around his ankles, and the flesh exposed between them and his trouser cuffs was pale yellow and not healthy-looking.

"Yes?" The voice, even in that one word, was a mellow rumble. No doubt he owed it the most of his votes.

I had intended launching into a long song and dance leading up to the main subject, but for some reason I changed my mind at the last second. I stood in the doorway, then turned and slid the double doors together before I faced him to answer.

I moved closer and looked him over slow, from toe to tip. I noticed he was beginning to come bald. "Trask," I said. Just the one word. Trask. I hadn't known what to expect. Maybe I should have guessed.

The judge had a face infused with red. Red veins close to the surface and whiskey-red in between. When I said Ben's name, though, the old man went dead pale. Just as quick as that, there wasn't a trace of color above his neck. Then nearly as quick he flushed red and half rose from the chair. It was easy to see he'd have been a powerful man in his prime and perhaps for a good while longer. Now the power had left him. The capacity to come to quick anger had not.

"Get out," he said. His face was so red I was scared he would have a stroke and die on the spot. "Tell him it won't work now. I have the original. Any copies he might have made will do him no good. I made sure of that. Now get out of here before I cane you."

He lumbered upright and stood towering over me, taller than I'd expected and as angry as I've ever seen a man. I switched quickly from my idea of trying to threaten this man into telling what I wanted to know.

"You have the wrong idea, Your Honor," I said. I let my face go hard. "I don't work for Trask. I want to kill him."

He looked at me for a long moment, then sat back into his chair. But now he was erect. No longer slouching there.

"Just like that?"

"I'd prefer a fair fight," I said.

"Why?"

"It's a long story. Are you willing to tell me yours first?" I didn't know what kind of a hold the Trasks must have had on the judge, but I didn't figure it would hurt any if he thought we were in the same boat.

He looked me up and down and I had my fingers crossed, in my mind anyway. My clothes were respectable enough. And if people could take me for a dummy, maybe they could take me for a sneak or a cheat as well. It was plain that the judge had been blackmailed, just like the telegraph operator had been. Well, maybe for a change my looks would be a help. Maybe I looked like someone capable of some trickery that would have left me open to blackmail too.

The judge shook his head. "I don't think my story would interest you," he said.

"Exactly. But we may have a common interest in other areas."

His Honor smiled broadly and with that his face came alive. He had force and presence of a sudden, when before he had seemed simply a fat old man. I may have made too much of his voice in the vote-getting process. "Indeed we may, sir." He shoved a huge, blunt-fingered hand toward me. "Hubert Eustace Hinsley, sir. Your servant."

"James Denton Williams, sir. And I am honored."

He nodded. "May I offer you a cup of wine, Mr. Williams? Beaujolais. Very nice, I believe."

"I would be delighted to join you, Your Honor." Oh, we was being polite, we were.

He bellowed. "Frances!" Within seconds the plump lady was at the door, this time without the dish towel. "A decanter and two goblets, Frances."

She was back practically as soon as she'd left, with a silver tray and a matching set of crystal decanter and glasses. The glasses were actually balloon snifters intended for brandy service, but the judge made no comment on it. She set the tray on a folding table next to his chair and left, drawing the doors closed behind her.

His Honor smiled. He poured the wine, passed me one, and took a deep swallow himself. Feeling right ceremonious about it, I raised my glass in his direction and took a sip. He was right. It was very nice stuff.

"And now, sir. How is it I could help you?"

"First, by telling me what you know about the Trasks. And secondly, by telling me where I might find them and a man named Joshua Davis."

Hinsley grunted. He placed his fingers together to form a tent and peered inside it. He looked back to me. "What do you want to know about . . . my own encounters with the Trask family?"

"Nothing you wouldn't tell any registered voter," I assured him. He went back into the tent, so to speak.

He grunted again. "I see no harm in discussing a mutual acquaintance, Mr. Williams. You understand, of course, that I know them only slightly and have never, myself, had any dealings with them whatsoever."

"Of course not, Your Honor," I said quickly. Ah yes, we understood each other nicely. "I understand that their integrity is . . . questionable. I would never dream of impugning your honor, personally or professionally, by implying that your good name could in any way be linked to theirs."

"Of course not. Never thought for a minute that you would, my boy." He grunted and shifted back in his chair to a more relaxed position. He assayed the level of my glass with a practiced eye and refilled his own almost to the brim. "Um, where should I begin now? I suppose with the father."

The judge talked. Long into the night. He had a good voice and a logical mind and a love for hearing himself talk, so I never once had to prompt him along once he got going. Before he was done we'd emptied the wine jug once and had a start on a second filling of it.

It seemed the Trask boys came by their ways in a natural manner. You might say they came by them honest, though the word doesn't much seem to apply in their case.

Their father had been a Mississippi riverboat rider. A far ranging, gamblin' man with big ambitions, Hinsley said he'd been. Though he didn't say how it was he'd come to know.

Anyway, Trask the Eldest—Hinsley never said his first name— met the boys' mother on a steam trip upriver from New Orleans. According to the old judge, Trask fell for this innocent and beautiful Southern belle in a real big way and vowed he'd change his wicked ways if only she'd accept him.

Nobody knew for sure any more, Hinsley said, but there was some speculation that her past might of been even more wicked than Trask's, though she had a genteel way about her and gave a virginal impression even with three growed sons standing behind her chair. What she'd hoped to gain through Trask, the judge said, was anybody's guess although he could believe anything, or near anything, that could be suggested.

Trask married the lady, gave up the riverboat life, and found himself being helped by his new bride in a series of shady land development schemes. It was some years back that they'd moved to an open range ranch east of Pueblo and began filing homestead claims and buying claims and inventing claimants until they had a nice-sized place, all under deeded ownership.

There was a neighbor, fella name of Cates, a widower who built his own place pretty much the same way except Cates was there first and had all the good water rights. Which didn't seem to mean a thing to the Trasks when they were acquiring their landholdings.

Now the judge did not try to draw any conclusions from this, but I could do some guessing on the subject. And land speculators would try to peddle anything that could be surveyed into impressive deed descriptions, while a cowman would be sorta choicy about giving his stock the grass and water they need to drop calves and to reach market weight.

A couple years ago the Trask family leader failed to return home from one of his business trips. I guess the judge had done a little checking on the subject. He said the eldest Trask sold some bottom land to an old boy from Minnesota who found out unexpected quick that his river had changed its channel thirty years or more before, leaving him high, dry, and dusty. The old boy punctuated his side of the discussion with a minie-ball from a two-dollar war surplus musket, .58 caliber and still potent after thirty years of hard use.

The widow had not seemed totally bereft by her loss. She received the news, put on her widow's weeds, fixed her hair extra neat, and went fishing. She caught what she was after, in the form of neighbor Cates.

As soon as the happy couple were united in wedded bliss, Hinsley said, the missus suggested they both sell out and move east where they could enjoy civilized surroundings together. Just why, the judge did not know. He said even with the water Cates had, the land was not of enough worth to set the woman up with a last score, so to speak. He said he did not understand that part of it.

And things had not been going well in the Cates family. A year ago Cates's son was taken sick. Died in bed with a flux of some sort and nothing anyone could do to stop its progress. Then there was the Cates girl. Her brother's death hit her so hard she lost her mind, poor thing. Hinsley told me about that with a clear eye and a steady, calm expression.

The boys would likely be found at the Cates place, due east about forty miles.

"What was the other name, son?" He took another swallow of his wine.

"Davis, Your Honor. Joshua Davis, it is."

"Name rings a bell with me, but I don't remember from where." Hinsley sat musing on the subject.

I sort of hated to be telling him where I'd been doing my reading of late, but I figured I had no choice. "It's in the order declaring Janet Cates feeble-minded, I believe."

He gave me a fast, sharp look. "Yes, I believe you are correct, sir. It was about . . . yes, it was about the guardianship. Something to do with that."

"The paper says something about Davis being a blood relative."

"A *blood* relative? Oh no. Couldn't be. Why, I've known little Janet's family since before she was born. Her daddy's been out here since the early mining days. Came out here with a shovel, made a small strike, and decided he'd rather work above the ground than in it. Smart man, Ezra Cates. And a good man. Shame about the children, though."

"But Davis?"

He shrugged, meaty shoulders raising heavily and making his vest shift on his belly. He was getting right tipsy. "I wouldn't know about Davis."

He extended the wine decanter again but I refused.

"You are leaving then?"

"Yes, sir. It is late. And I have much to do."

"Ah yes. You mentioned something about that earlier. Not, you understand, that I would condone anything beyond the exact letter of the law."

"Certainly not, Your Honor."

"And is there anything I should know about you, Mr. Williams?"

"No, sir. I would say there is not."

"Somehow I expected precisely that answer," he said with a smile. "But no matter. Having foreseen it, I could not now complain about my own accuracy."

The judge rose ponderously to his feet and carefully fastened every button on the vest before he extended his hand to me. "Good luck to you, sir."

"And to you, Your Honor." And I meant it. Whatever he had done in the past to make him vulnerable to the Trask boys, I hoped it would not be repeated. "Good night to you, sir."

CHAPTER 19

The Cates ranch headquarters lay along both sides of a narrow, pretty stream lined with overhanging willows. From a distance it looked more like a small town than a single ranch.

The main house was huge. Two-storied and white-painted, with single story lean-to wings sprawling out around it. It had the look of a home lived with as well as lived in. A wide veranda across the front of the place was cluttered with rocking chairs and dogs, but the chairs were all pushed neatly back against the wall. It may have been only my own prejudices showing through, but I got the idea maybe they were not being used much these days.

Around it and lined out on both sides of the stream were the other buildings. Barns, stock pens, smokehouse, icehouse. Several bunkhouses, laundry, tack sheds, feed storage, smithy, machinery sheds with the green and red gleam of mowers and swathers seen through open doors. There were tidy small houses for the married employees and canvas-covered mountains of new hay ready for winter feeding.

Cates's operation had the look of one run by a good stockman and by a good businessman as well. The ranch garden to feed all these people covered several acres in a single plot, obviously tended by someone who would have to have that as his or her principal job. There were several pens of hogs and a large flock of laying hens. An orchard covered a small flat with irrigation ditches branching from the stream. The place seemed like it should be darn well self-sufficient.

There were few people in evidence as I approached, most of them Mexican women idling from one outbuilding to the next. A squat, balding Mexican with thigh-thick arms and sweat streaming down his face pounded industriously on an anvil at the smithy. Lounging in a swing under a half-dead cottonwood was a lean old boy with a chew in his cheek, a battered John B. on his head, and a leg strapped up tight in splints. I reined the mule to a halt before him.

"Looks like you stayed with one a mite longer than you ought to've," I observed.

He spit and grinned at me. "Truth is, the ride was a jump or two short." He looked me over, and I guess I passed inspection. I was back in comfortable clothes, and they were a little new but plenty dusty by now. "I s'pose you're like everyone else around here. Never before heard of a man bein' throwed."

I scratched the stubble on my jaw—I deliberately hadn't shaved that morning when I let the Grande—and said, "No-o-o-o. That ain't really so. Heard once about a boy being throwed. I think it was somewhere around Uvalde, Texas. Back around '72, I think it was."

"Sure am glad to hear that," he said. "I been feelin' awful lonesome the last few days. Get down an' set if you like," he said with a wave of one hand.

I stepped down and dropped the mule's reins to ground-tie him. I hunkered down and picked up a twig to scrape around in the dust by my feet.

"Winter crew's filled," he said around his chew.

"I figured."

"Might take somebody on short time," he said.

"Who's the man to see?"

"Foreman's name is Jess Wilford. He'll be in come evenin'."

"Who's the boss?"

"The foreman is. For right now anyhow."

"Company ranch, is it?"

"Naw. Man name of Cates owns it lock, stock 'n' barrel. But he's laid up over to th' big house with some sort of flux." He spat. "I don't 'spect we'll see him again outside of a box."

"Shame."

"So it is. Same thing took his boy a couple year ago. An' his girl disappeared. Run off with some man or sumthin'. Reckon he's got no good reason to hang on longer."

Now that statement jolted me, and my head come up quick. I looked at the man close. "Seems a lonesome way to die," I said.

He shrugged. "Ain't they all?" I scratched in the dust some more, my head down lest he get too good a look at the expression that might be leaking through onto my face. "Still," the fellow went on, "he's had more troubles than most of late. Lost his wife, then the boy, an' now the girl gone too. That one s'prised me, she did. Always figured her for a solid one, ever since she stood no higher than a stirrup."

"You been here a while then?"

"I have." There was considerable pride in his voice. "No better man to ride for than Ez Cates." He shook his head. "That might be over too, now."

"Oh?"

"I don't make no secret of the way I feel 'bout things. I ain't fond of the new missus an' her boys. Don't know that I'd want to ride for them should Ezra an' his family be gone. Wouldn't be the same at all."

"Good man can always find work," I said.

"Long as there's cows an' horses, there'll be need for men an' ropes," he agreed.

"You rope as good as you ride?" I poked at him.

"Maybe even better," he said with a straight face. "Dabbed a loop onto a Joshua tree once down in Arizona. Big ol' thing. Pulled it smack over onto the horse. Got him a rump full of spines. If I'd had money placed on him ahead of time, I'd be a rich man today."

I nodded, serious as could be. "Know what you mean. I roped a snake once. Still in its hole. It curled up in a ball and wouldn't come loose. Horse spooked and fetched out the snake an' a pile of dirt ten feet acrost an' twenty feet deep. My saddle partner seen color down to the bottom of it an' staked out his claim. He come out of it with a big house an' a private railroad car. Me, I got a snakeskin hatband."

The old boy spat and scratched himself. "Once when I was

down in Phoenix I met a man could throw a square loop. We got to talkin' an' come up with a wager. He said . . ."

" 'Scuse me," I butted in, and jumped to my feet. I slipped the thong loose from the hammer of my old Remington. The old boy looked around. Just come out of one of the big barns was Tom Trask. There was no way he could miss seeing me and that gray mule standing under a shade tree in his own yard.

"You got troubles with Tommy?" the Cates rider asked in a low voice.

"I think I'm about to have."

"Whew-ee," the old boy said. "You sure picked the wrong place to be lookin' for work. That boy's about as full of poison as his brothers. I reckon he took it to you?"

"Him an' Ben did. Long story, though." I was talking to this fellow beside me, but my eyes hadn't left Tom. "Is Ben here too?"

"Not lately. Tom's the onliest one right now. Don't know where Ben an' Leo have got to."

"I appreciate knowin' that."

"Aw, they're bad, them boys. But I can't imagine anybody comin' up behind your back if that's what's worryin' you."

I took my eyes off Tom long enough to smile at him. "I'll show you my scars sometime, courtesy of Ben and his brothers. The holes start at the back."

"Interestin', that is," he said.

"I thought so."

"I take it you weren't much interested in work, after all."

"I will admit I got a little tired of being run at by those boys."

Tom had seen me now. He altered direction toward me, and a wide, happy smile spread across his face. His teeth were as white and even as Ben's, his smile just as engaging. Oh, these was likeable, easygoing boys.

"It is good to see you again, Stumpy," he said when he was close enough. "We heard you were out of jail."

"I'll bet you was just overjoyed."

"You know," he mused, "Ben almost *was* glad. But now he'll be unhappy again. I will get to do something he wanted for himself."

"You'll have to earn the privilege, Tommy."

The stove-up cowhand's eyes were bouncing from one of us back to the other as we spoke.

"I'm not much worried about that, Stumpy. Not at all, in fact." I shrugged. "Like I said. Your privilege if you can earn it, but mighty tough potatoes if you can't."

"You did give us some surprises before, Stumpy. Who'd ever guess that a dumb old cowboy would turn out to be a respectable cowman? But I don't think that matters now. Now we're getting into my line of the family business."

"Now that Leo isn't around to handle the chores for you?"

Tom flushed. "I've never had to hold second candle."

The cowhand was looking uneasy. I don't think he'd ever seen this side of the Trask boys before. He couldn't be understanding all that was said, but the gist of it was plain enough.

I smiled at Tom. "Well, boy, I've come out all right against Leo and not so bad against Ben. Shall we see how poor, dumb ol' Stumpy does with you?"

"Believe me, I'm looking forward to it."

"Yeah. That's why you sprung spang into action right the first minute you seen me. You boys are talkative, ain't you?"

Tom got redder. He was commencing to get mad, and I didn't mind that a bit. The muddier his mind got, the more I'd like it.

"Where's Miss Janet?" I said quickly, hoping to throw him out of gear a little further. "Where does Josh Davis live?"

Tom glanced quickly at the cowhand, still sitting in the swing and obviously wondering what all this was we were talking about. The mention of Miss Janet had really got his attention, and that seemed to worry Tom.

Tom straightened. His right wrist stiffened, and his fingers began to curl into so many hooks ready to grasp the butt of the shiny Colt he wore tied to his leg. I grinned, mocking him. My right hand hung loose beside my revolver. It did not please him.

All right. I will admit to being wound tight inside, with as much tension on me as a rawhide reata caught between a thousand-pound steer and a hard-driving cow pony. But I knew it wouldn't pay to harden those muscles before time and maybe let unnecessary fatigue enter into the picture.

Tom was ready to pull, working himself up to whatever push it was he needed to make the move. Then, from toward the main house, there was the distinctive creak and slam of a screen door being opened. Tom's eyes shifted that way and instead of coming back to me his attention stayed somewhere beyond my right shoulder. His arm relaxed and the tight bend fell out of his wrist.

"What are you doing there, Thomas?" It was a woman's voice, a very full and rich voice.

She stopped beside Tom, a stately, even elegant woman dressed as if for the city. There was the merest smattering of gray in her piled and tight wound hair. I took it that this was the Widow Trask, now the respected wife of Ezra Cates.

"What are you doing, Thomas?" she demanded again. There was authority in her tone, and I don't doubt that I would have answered as quick as Tom.

"Our visitor is that Williams fellow Ben told you about," he said.

She turned her head and the lines of her throat and neck looked positively regal. Her posture was as straight as a West Point colonel inspecting his cadets. She looked at me with all the interest and respect one would give to a new variety of scorpion observed on your parlor wall.

"Do you mean to tell me that this misshapen creature is the one capable of annoying my Benjamin?" I never heard a colder voice come out of anything human.

"Yes, Mama, but I was about to take care of that when you joined us. I'll be glad to tend to it, Mama." There was an eagerness in Tom's voice that saddened me and made me feel sorry for him in spite of everything. It was an eagerness not for blood but for approval. It told me perhaps more than I'd wanted to know about the Trasks. Or at least about Tom.

"See that you do it then, Thomas."

"Yes, Mama." He pointed a thumb toward the Cates rider. "Sid's been with us the whole time. Should he go back into the bunkhouse?"

"Certainly not," she said. "It will be good for him to witness everything that happens here." She hiked her nose a good three inches higher. "I do not want it said that a Trask took unfair advantage or engaged in anything but the most honorable of affairs. Sid can assure the other hands, and anyone else who might inquire, that this was exactly the case here."

I mean, when you think about it, this woman was sorta silly. Here she was, talking about how her rider could tell about my death. And me standing there listening to it.

"If it's all the same to you, ma'am," I said with a deliberately exaggerated drawl, "I will go ahead an' defend myself before you bury me." She gave me a look that I believe a lady would describe as being withering and turned to go. I guess I didn't feel much like being withered. I put my attention on Tom.

Tom watched his mama go back into the house. We could hear the creak and slap of the screen door again. Tom's eyes were big, open to the depths of him, and when he looked back my way I felt a surge of sympathy for him, an impulse to tell him it would be all right if only he wouldn't try so awful hard to please her. To tell him we could sit and talk and go our separate ways with no hard feelings.

But the idea was stillborn. What could I say that would not reflect harshly on the man's mother? And how could he listen to any truths about her? We neither one of us had any choice.

"You wouldn't settle for a fistfight, would you, Tom?" It was the best I could manage under the circumstances.

"I couldn't," he said. He meant it, too. Just exactly that. He couldn't. Not after his mama had made it plain he was to kill me. "Maybe you understand that, huh?"

"Sure, Tom. I understand," I said softly. And I held no hate for this boy. I like to think he knew that.

"How about if Sid gives a signal to make things square?" he asked.

"Fine," I said. My eyes stayed on Tom, though I was not expecting any tricks from him. Not here. Not with his mama watching and him wanting to impress her with how good he could do what she wanted. "Sid," I said, "whenever you're ready, snap your fingers."

Tom's arm and wrist were again poised and taut, his hand bent at the wrist and fingers hooked. He was the very picture of a fast draw artist. Me, I was standing loose but ready, upright while Tom crouched like he was ready to leap.

The broken-legged cowboy snapped his fingers, and Tom's hand jerked up, clawing for the butt of his pretty Colt.

I had no choice about it. I palmed the old Remington and let her roll. The cylinder bellowed and turned and the stocks bucked in my big, misshapen hand, and I loosed three shots into Thomas.

The first caught him just above the belt; the second took him square in the chest. The final slug, the barrel still rising as I fought the recoil of the big .44-40, took him somewhere in the face. I never looked afterward to see exactly where. His gun was out of the leather, ending up laying beside him in the dirt.

"I thought Tom was supposed to be pretty fast," the cowboy said. He was still sitting in his swing.

"Tom thought Tom was fast," I said. I glanced at him and saw that flies were already starting to find the fresh blood. It was more than I wanted to see. I turned back to the Cates rider.

"Listen, there's no way I can go calling in that house now," I said. "Can you get in to talk to Ezra Cates?"

"Sure, but why?" He looked a little suspicious.

"It's a long story an' you wouldn't have any good reason to believe me even if I told it all. An' I gotta get away from here pretty quick. The thing is, Miss Janet—you heard me an' Tom mention her—Miss Janet never run off from nobody nor with anybody. The Trask boys got a court order sayin' she's feeble-minded and got her locked up." That idea drew a snort from the man.

"Anyway, she can't get loose to come home. I don't know what it's all about, but she needs help. And her papa needs to be alive when I get her back here."

"If you're right, mister, I'll tell Ez an' round up a crew to come with you."

"Are the hands here trustworthy? Cates riders from a ways back?"

"Well, a lot of the boys is new, but . . ."

"Never you mind then. I don't want any chances taken with this. Not when a few bullets could get rid of everyone who might be able to help the girl. You talk to Cates, and I'll go to looking for a place owned by a man name of Joshua Davis."

"Josh Davis. I know him. He's a brother to the missus. Miz Cates, that is. Why, twice a year now he borrows Cates riders on the Cates payroll to make his roundups. Awful tight with a nickel, that man. Wouldn't spend one to watch a pissant eat a bale of hay."

We'd spent overlong talking. The screen door slammed.

"I gotta ride. Where's the Davis place?"

"About ten mile east to a dry creek bed. Follow that south about twenty mile more to a permanent stream. Follow upstream four mile to Davis' place."

"I thank you, neighbor." I gathered up the reins of the mule and took to running. The Widow Trask had a long gun in her hands, and I wanted to shoot no woman.

CHAPTER 20

I rode away, feeling no elation at what I left behind. It was just a thing that'd had to be done. Now I was looking forward to the rest of it. Miss Janet would almost certainly be at that Davis ranch.

The mule covered ground at an even, rapid pace that was so comfortable to set. It was no trouble to find the dry run creek east of Cates's place and follow down it the way the cowhand had said. It was coming dark when I got to the live water, so I pulled up there.

I stripped the gear from the mule and rubbed him down. He seemed to like the feel of it and the attention both. He ate from a sack of oats I'd lashed behind the saddle, and I ate from a sack that'd been tied on the other side. I think both of us felt better when we'd finished. I sat for a time peeling hulls from some left-over oat grains and nibbling at the plump, soft meats. Then I curled up with a blanket under me. I wanted a good rest before I went calling upstream.

I slept well enough. It was good to be out in the open again after so long with roofs and walls and too soft beds. Not that they weren't nice in their place, but enough was enough. It just felt good to be tasting clean air and live water.

Morning found me in a good humor, and I believe Gray felt just as good. He brayed and flipped his ratty little bit of mule tail and seemed to be saying how pretty the morning was. The sky was twenty shades of violet and the birds were tuning up their voices when we moved off upstream.

We hustled right along and it was just like I'd hoped. We got to the Davis ranch right at breakfast time. We rode straight to

the bunkhouse door and I put on the traditional look of the grub-
line rider, a sort of half-shy grin that was accepted as meaning
Gee, fellas, it's mealtime and I'm hungry.

The Davis place was about what I'd expected from what
Cates's rider had said. The main house was low-roofed and un-
painted, slapped together with rough lumber and used nails—or
else by a man who couldn't drive a new nail straight and just
clinched over the bent ones from laziness. The bunkhouse was
worse. I expect it would have been real comfortable in the summer, with a fresh breeze passing through all the time, but I
wouldn't want to winter there. There were a few sagging out-
buildings and some pens, but no barn. And the new hay was piled
in the open where some of it was sure to sour before the next
spring's grass was up.

Haying and winter feeding were something we'd have to study
on, I was thinking. As far south as we were, we'd never had to
worry about it before. I'd already read enough to know that people up here never used to winter feed either, but the big die-up
had taught most of them the value of hay.

Thinking like that, about all the things we would have to do to
establish a new ranch in Utah, I found that I'd started whistling
to myself. Gray's big ears were cocked back in my direction. They
swiveled forward when a man came to the bunkhouse door.

"Hope you haven't flung your leavin's to the dogs yet," I said
politely, and took my hat off. Also traditional.

The man nodded. "There's enough," he said. "Light and set."
He was a stocky man with a patch of dense fur showing at the
throat of his shirt. He might have been the foreman, cook, a
waddy or Davis himself. He didn't offer to say who or what he
was.

I stepped off Gray and the man directed me to one of the pens.
There was no tack shed handy so I hung my kak on the top rail
with four other scarred and much used saddles. I guess it was a
convenient arrangement but a little hard on a man's rig.

I went back to the bunkhouse and the man hooked a thumb toward the main house. "Chow's over there. Soon as they bang the

iron." He disappeared into the bunkhouse without suggesting I join him. Or them. Or whatever.

There was a log split in half lengthwise and fitted with legs to form a bench and set beside the doorway. I made myself comfortable on it and tried to keep occupied by admiring the horseflesh in Davis' pens. It was not easy to do. They were not very admirable horses.

There weren't but two or three that were more than a single, slim level above Glen Maxfield's cull mustangs. I'd have hated to tie into any heavy beef with one of them under my saddle. There were few enough of them, too. Either the crew was awful short-stringed or there wasn't much of a crew. Maybe both.

It wasn't long before I found out. About the time the sun was separating itself from the horizon—plenty late by our standards down home—the breakfast gong went to clanging, and four men came clattering out of the bunkhouse, one of them the man I'd spoken to before. "Come along," he said as he passed, so I trailed along in the rear of the procession.

We went into the main house through a side door, to a long, narrow room that was nearly filled by a long, narrow table. Much too much table for a crew this size. There was a man already seated at the kitchen end of the table. Davis, I figured.

He was a thin, scruffy sort in a soiled shirt and wearing galluses instead of a belt, common enough in town but a little unusual here. I don't believe I would have taken to him much even if I hadn't been prejudiced against him before I ever saw him. He just struck me that way.

The woman who was loading the table was a thin, pale thing. Even the hair pulled into a tiny bun at the nape of her neck was thin and pale. The material of her loose, hanging dress looked as if it had been washed a time or two too often. It needed more patching than it had gotten.

If this was Davis' missus, and I got the impression she was, it could maybe explain the late start to the day. It would be quite a job for one woman to handle everything that would need doing. Or maybe Davis was plain lazy. His operation sure indicated he might be that as well as cheap.

We sat down to table and everyone began reaching without any exchange of morning pleasantries.

I was pleased to find that the platters and bowls were well filled, but I noticed that the fare was limited. Griddle cakes, fried potatoes, oatmeal, and a huge tureen of scrambled eggs. All stuff that could be fed in large amounts on the cheap. No meat, no pies, no canned fruits. We'd have been butchering our stock cows before we laid a table without meat on it.

No one offered objections, though. In fact, no one said a word during the entire meal. The men ate quickly, Mrs. Davis keeping the food and coffee coming and not sitting down with us herself.

When the meal was over Davis got up and trooped out with his riders. He gave me a come-along look that I pretended not to notice. I was lingering over another cup of the hot, strong coffee.

As soon as the men were gone I began picking up dirty plates and carrying the stuff into the kitchen at the rear of the house. Like I'd expected, there was no one in there to help with the cleaning up.

"Be glad to take a hand with the dryin' towel, ma'am," I told Mrs. Davis when everything was proper stacked beside a copper sink.

She shot a harried, nervous glance out the window toward the horse pens and another, even quicker, toward a door leading to somewhere in the house. "I could use some water," she said in a voice so soft I could scarce hear it.

I picked up the two metal buckets she kept at the sink and went out a back door to the well. The well was not situated as good as one might like. It was about forty yards from the back stoop, and the water was far down in the shaft. It took considerable cranking to fetch a bucket to the top. I carried the full buckets back to the house, the wire bales cutting into my hands, and thought how much easier on the woman a yoke would be. But it was not my place to suggest it.

When I got back with the water, the woman had started washing. I grabbed a towel and set to drying, something I hadn't done in years, what with a family running long on womenfolk.

The first thing I picked up was a small, battered bowl made of tin. I hadn't seen anything like that when the dishes were stacked.

"Where'd this come from?" I asked in a friendly, curious tone.

The woman looked startled. "I just . . . I just gave our hound some scraps," she said hesitantly.

"Uh-huh," I said. I laid the towel down. There'd been plenty of time for Davis to ride out with his hands. And I didn't much care if he hadn't. "Ma'am?"

"Yes?" Her voice was thin, tired.

"I've come to take Miss Janet home, ma'am."

She looked at me, and there was a flash of savage pleasure in those pale, watery eyes. "Good." It was more hiss than word. "Take her. Take her quick. He can't say anything if you done it."

She wiped her hands dry on her apron and plucked at my sleeve. "I'll show you where."

The woman led me through the door off the kitchen into a narrow, dark hallway. About halfway down there was an alcove on the right with a latched trapdoor set in the floor. The woman opened the catch and lifted the heavy door, propping it open against the back wall. A ladder led down into darkness below the house. A heavy, damp, cellar odor came through the opening.

From a shelf I hadn't noticed in the gloom, the woman took candle and matches. She lit the candle and handed it to me. "The girl's down there," she said.

I looked at her for a moment, hesitant about entering that uncertain opening with her still above. And possibly her husband or even Ben Trask as well. She seemed to know what I would be thinking. She took the candle from me and led the way down the ladder.

There was a packed earth floor and unmortared stone walls in the cellar and apparently no other way in or out. The walls were lined with shelving, bare now and with light circles in their dust coating showing where large stocks of canned foods had been stored until fairly recently. At the other side of the cellar in the farthest fringe of candlelight there was a hint of motion.

Mrs. Davis moved in that direction and the light, nearer, showed Miss Janet seated on a wood bunk much like the one I'd used so much in Apishapa City. In the jail there.

Miss Janet was dressed the same as I'd last seen her except now her clothes were greasy with filth. Her hair had a greasy, stringy look to it too but was tied at the back of her neck to keep it in some semblance of order. Her face was smeared with dirt and her hands were filthy. Her fingers shone with moisture from something, and of a sudden I realized that they'd been making her eat without utensils of any sort. She was not a pretty sight. Yet her chin was held high and defiant. "What do you want now?" she demanded, with no hint of fear or hesitation in her voice.

The woman stepped to the side and held the candle higher. I guess Mrs. Davis' body had screened most of its light from me. I will always be glad that I was watching the girl's face when she seen me there. It put value to all the things that'd been happening of late.

From being set and unbending, Miss Janet's expression ripped through a whole series of changes, just that quick. Shock. Surprise. Hope. Delight. Of course it would have been the same for anyone who'd come to help her. I didn't try to tell myself different. But I was awful glad it was me got to see it happen.

She cried out, "Stumpy," and before I knew it she was on her feet and had me around the neck, purely overcome with joy.

"Yes, ma'am," I whispered, and I guess my eyes were a little wetter than they ought to have been.

The arms around my neck were terrible thin and her weight against me was no more than so much smoke. Still there was no question that she was a girl, and I felt my face heating up like a coal-fired stove.

She lifted her head away from my throat where it'd been nestled and wrinkled her nose. "I'll bet I smell awful."

I couldn't help but grin. "Yes, ma'am. You do."

"But oh, I don't care; I don't care." She let go of me and pirouetted on the dirt floor. "I can change that now, can't I, Stumpy?"

"Yes'm. You can do anything you want now. Pretty soon anyway."

"You better go now, mister, afore my man comes back," Mrs.

Davis said. Her voice was stronger, braver than it had been before.

"Is there anything you need to take with you?"

Miss Janet's laugh was short and bitter. "Nothing but what I'm wearing."

"Let's go then. Before there's trouble."

I went up the ladder first, the thong slipped free of my revolver. Mrs. Davis waited at the bottom with the candle and came up last. We went into the kitchen and Miss Janet blinked and squinted against the unaccustomed brightness, even indoors like that.

Miss Janet looked at Mrs. Davis with a funny sort of awkward look. I thought I could understand why. This was a woman who'd participated in what was a virtual captivity of the girl. Yet now Mrs. Davis had very obviously helped me take the girl out of that cellar.

"Could I have a drink of water, please?" Miss Janet asked.

"Sure, honey." Mrs. Davis jumped to get her a cup of water from one of the buckets I'd carried in. She also sliced a couple thick slabs off a loaf of bread and smeared them thick with butter. "You better take these too."

"Yes." Miss Janet looked at the woman for a long moment, then turned away. I guess there really wasn't much they could have said to each other. Miss Janet went out onto the back stoop.

I paused a moment before I followed her. "I'll be taking one of the mister's horses," I told the woman. "I'll have someone bring it back later." She nodded.

Miss Janet was standing outside with her face uplifted, breathing deep of the clean, free air. I knew I could not fully appreciate what she was feeling. A jail cell had been nothing compared to that dark, close cellar.

I touched her on the arm, and she smiled. "Can I go home now, Stumpy?"

"Yes, ma'am. I think your daddy would like that just fine."

CHAPTER 21

The closer we got to her home the brighter Miss Janet's eyes got and the happier she looked. When we got near she threw an eager laugh at me over her shoulder and kicked Gray into action. I was bareback on Davis' bronc and had an uncomfortable time trying to stay with her. As it was she swept into the ranch yard well ahead of me.

She was out of the saddle and into the house with her skirts a-flying. I pulled the bronc down to a much more comfortable walk and took my time getting on up to the house front.

I slid off the animal and he took that last opportunity to try and cow-kick me. I shoved clear of him and let the reins drop to the ground. I didn't know if the ornery beast was trained to ground-tie, but I didn't much care. It was Davis' horse and Davis' bridle. If the thing wanted to take off cross-country for home now, it was all right with me.

I stood on the veranda for a moment, wondering if I should barge in unasked, and finally decided I'd better. I didn't know who all might be in there, and if there was going to be trouble I wanted to be handy.

The screen door announced my entry with its loud spring squeal, and I eased it shut behind me.

The entry was made of varnished and highly polished wood. There were wooden pegs on the side wall for hats and coats, but the pegs were empty now. Well, that only meant there wasn't company in the house.

Ahead of the small entry foyer was a sort of usable hall-like area with a piano next to some stairs leading upward. There were a couple wooden benches—but nice made stuff with fancy carving, not rough furniture by any stretch of the imagination—with long, velvet-covered pillows for upholstering. Flanking either side of a set of sliding double doors to the right were a pair of small tables with tops inlaid with polished marble shapes. Each of them held a tall vase full of peacock feathers.

I took a look into the parlor. The walls were papered in a pretty rose print. It was full of heavily stuffed furniture and tables and footstools and lamps with painted globes and heavy draperies—all of it arranged so you could enjoy a drink or some conversation by the big, stone-manteled fireplace. Even at this time of year there was pinyon wood laid ready for the touch of a match.

I wasn't sure where to look for Miss Janet and her daddy, then I heard voices and the slam of a door upstairs. Someone said something in a sharp voice. Then several someones were shouting. Women's voices. I grinned. I had an idea the Widow Trask was very disappointed in her boys.

A door slammed, and I heard the clatter of feet on stairs though no one came down the stairway to the hall where I was. There was a screen door slam from the rear of the house.

It sounded like things were straightening themselves out up there, so I made myself comfortable on one of those padded benches and waited. It was quite a while before Miss Janet remembered me and came downstairs.

"I'm so happy, Stumpy," she said, which was pretty obvious without her saying so. "Please come up and meet my father. There is so much we have to thank you for."

"Yes'm. I'd be glad to."

Cates was propped up against a mound of soft pillows on a big, canopied bed. He looked emaciated, and his color was not good. But from the look on his face he felt just fine now. He extended his hand, and I was real proud to shake it.

"J. D. Williams, sir, and very happy to make your acquaintance."

"Your name has figured rather prominently in Janet's conversation the last few minutes, Mr. Williams," he said. He was a stockman and had been a miner once, but there was an almost courtly dignity to this man. It was easy to understand Miss Janet's quality, with a father like this.

"I must say I am shocked," he went on, "but it is obvious that we have much to thank you for." He shook his head. "Not that I was as completely surprised as I might have been, and I believe I have you to thank for that also. Sid Hames, one of my riders, paid me a visit yesterday evening. There was much going on here of which I had been completely unaware. And I still do not understand why."

"If you would forgive a blunt statement, sir, I would suggest that the answer would be simple greed somewhere in the picture," I said.

"I heard Ben talking with Mr. Davis," Miss Janet said. She was still filthy dirty, but she looked awfully perky and nice, setting close by her daddy on the edge of his bed. "I didn't understand what they said, but it had something to do with railroad shares. But for now, if you gentlemen will excuse me, I will leave that subject to you. I must bathe and find decent clothes before I attract an infestation of flies into the house." She popped up and gave her father a quick kiss on the cheek. She favored me with a bright smile and left the room in a lilting walk with echoes of a merry hop, skip, and a jump in it.

There was a world of affection in her father's look as she went. "She's all I have left, Williams," he said. "And to think that I came so close to losing her and never even knew it." He sighed and said, "It was difficult enough when I thought she had run away with some young man. The worst part of all this is that I was capable of believing such a thing about her."

Cates turned back toward me. "Greed, you say."

"It was my impression, sir."

"Tell me about your involvement in this and what you know of my . . . stepsons. I would like to know how your opinion was formed."

"All right, sir." I gave it a moment of thought before I began. I did not especially want to rattle off all my woes before this man. Yet he had a right to information as complete, as accurate, and as unbiased as I could give him. So I went ahead and told him, as briefly as I could without minimizing things for the sake of his feelings. After all, it was his own family I was discussing. And perhaps, still, the future of his only daughter.

When I was done I told him, "That is about it, Mr. Cates. You can see that I might be some prejudiced against the Trask family, but that is as straight as I could tell it."

He was silent for some time, and I could see that his thoughts would be hard ones. When he spoke it was back on the earlier question. "And you believe the motivation was—or is—greed, you said."

"I do, sir. It is strictly an impression. A guess, if you will. But I can't deny that I feel it strongly. Especially after my discussion with the good judge over in Pueblo."

"Yes. *Him*."

"Yes, sir, but to be fair, the man *was* coerced into his action."

"I still don't understand, Williams, how my . . . my wife or her sons would stand to gain. Even if I were to die, they would not benefit. My will—and they know of it—leaves my property to my children. If they were to die before me as . . . as my son did . . . then the ranch would be sold for the benefit of Oxford College." His mood lightened a bit when he observed my reaction to that, and I am sure he knew what I was thinking. "The one in Georgia, that is. East of Atlanta."

He became serious again. "So you can see that harming Janet would NOT enhance the fortunes of either my wife or her sons."

I thought on that a while. Then I realized. "But of course. That's just the thing, isn't it? Why all the trouble to have Miss Janet remain alive but legally an incompetent? Under the legal control of someone, Davis, completely in their control. Why else make the girl suffer and yet remain alive and a potential danger to them? And, my word, your illness came at a most convenient time. When Miss Janet *was* alive to inherit yet unable to take a voice in any matter. You coming down with a flux at just this time, the same as your son did, and . . ."

My voice trailed away. In the excitement of speculation and possible discovery I had forgotten the terrible, twisting emotions my words could cause within this man.

Cates had been pale before. Now his face was totally devoid of color.

"Excuse me, sir," I said quickly. "And, please . . . Forgive me." I got out of there as quickly as I could.

I'd spent an uncomfortable night as a guest under the Cates roof, but there had been no graceful escape. I had breakfast in the main house, too. With Miss Janet. Mrs. Cates, the former Widow Trask, was not in residence at the moment.

The girl was really lovely. It was the first time I'd seen her any way but dirty and in rough clothing. Now she was in her element, and all the promise of her was fulfilled and more. I had to take a firm hold of myself. It would not do for me to be thinking anything about this fine girl. She would never look at an ugly thing such as me, not a girl like this. I'd learned it early enough and often enough in the past. It would not do to forget it now.

Miss Janet was dressed in a sort of high-necked dress of a deep burgundy color with long sleeves buttoned close at the wrists but puffed at her shoulders. There was a froth of white lace at her throat. Her hair was glossy clean, piled in gleaming swirls at the back of her head and fastened there with a bunch of pearl-headed pins. There was a faint blush of color in her cheeks and her eyes were clear and wide and lovely.

I quit paying attention to her, or tried to anyhow, and put my mind on a solid breakfast of fried ham and fried potatoes, a pile of fried eggs, hominy, biscuits with a comb of honey, fresh apple pie and another pie made with canned peaches. I tried some of it all and enjoyed every bit of it.

When my plate was clean for the second or third time I leaned back with a sigh of contentment. The girl was sitting and watching me. She'd been through for some time and seemed to find my appetite amusing.

"Ma'am, you surely do have a fine cook. Please tell her I said so."

Her eyes were a-sparkle. "You already have. And I thank you most kindly, Mr. Williams."

"It'll be a lucky man that you decide on, ma'am."

"Again, thank you."

"You always do the cookin' around here, ma'am?"

She laughed. "Of course not. But I do enjoy it, and it has been quite a while since I've had a chance to cook for my father."

"Sure. How is your father this morning?"

"As a matter of fact, he is very much improved. I suppose that . . . tends to support the theory you proposed last night."

"He told you about that, then. I really feel bad about blurting it out without thinking beforehand," I said.

"There is no need for you to. You were expressing an honest opinion. Perhaps a correct one. Papa wants to talk with you about it when you've finished your breakfast."

"I'll go up to him right away then."

Cates was propped in his bed again. There was a wide, short-legged tray or bed table sort of thing beside him, loaded with dirty dishes and the remnants of a breakfast that must have been as big as mine, near about.

He looked me over when I entered. I'd dressed in my good clothes again, thinking maybe he would pay more attention to my ideas if I didn't look quite so much like a saddle tramp.

"Good morning, Williams," he said. His voice was cordial enough but his expression was serious. He motioned toward a chair beside the bed, so I took it.

"I've been thinking about what you said last night," he said right off the bat. "You may be right. I have talked with our cook and find that my wife has been preparing my meals without assistance of late. It is something Janet likes to do on occasion, but it is . . . highly unusual for Mrs. Cates to do so. Or had been until recently. It might be possible that my illness, and my son's earlier, could have been induced, well, unnaturally.

"Once I accepted that as a possibility I began thinking of other recent things, and some not so recent, that I had taken to be of no importance. I may have been mistaken."

"Yes, sir?"

"Last night Janet said she overheard Ben say something to Davis about railroad shares. I remember my wife, not long after we were married, talked to me about railroads. She wanted me to invest in a new railroad issue. I explained that Colorado railroads have a history of bringing their investors to grief. She said something about railroads being . . . let me remember . . . I believe she said the problem here was that railroad men had tried to take their profit from operating a railroad, while the real potential was in land grants along rights of way. I explained further that we hadn't money enough to form a railroad, even if I were interested. Which I was not. And that was the end of the subject. She never brought it up again."

He stopped and lay in the bed, his gaze turned inward. I waited for him to continue.

"A little more than a year ago, I received a rather generous offer for the purchase of our combined ranch. The offer was made by an English syndicate. My wife was willing to accept. I was not. The matter was dropped." Again he stopped to think. The next words came hard for him. "It was not long after that when . . . Ronnie took sick."

"It sounds real possible, doesn't it?"

"Yes, it does," he said. "But what a terrible thing."

"If I understand everything correctly, then, the whole idea was all a prelude to the real scheme in land speculation. Gain control of your ranch and sell it, along with their own land, to the Englishmen. Then use that money to capitalize a railroad stock issue, secure title to thousands of sections, maybe, of government grant land that they'd have the expertise to promote for a really big score, enough to set them up for life."

"You understand it quite well, Mr. Williams. Quite well indeed."

"Maybe so, sir. But proving it may be another matter completely. I don't think you would get any public co-operation from Judge Hinsley. And he's about all you've got for confirmation of your theory."

"I'm afraid I have come to the same conclusion, Williams."

"What next, then?"

"Several things, for one of which I must ask your help."

"Of course, sir. I'll do anything I possibly can."

"I believe my men can handle things here. I am aware of the

. . . the dangers now. I do not think I need worry too much about attempts on my life. And of course I shall take steps to . . . have my marriage dissolved. It seems the only sensible thing to do at this point. What concerns me most, however, is Janet's well being. And that is where you can help.

"Apparently the judge who issued that commitment order is willing to listen to you. I would like you to have that order rescinded and to explain the situation to enough county authorities to remove any further danger to her."

"Why, I'd be tickled to do that, Mr. Cates. I can leave right away if you like."

"The sooner it is ended, the safer Janet will be."

"I agree, sir. I'll do everything I can." He held out his hand and looked real appreciative. But it wasn't him I was doing it for.

CHAPTER 22

I came into Pueblo past the railroad station, but I didn't dwell on the thoughts that produced. I was thinking more about the way Miss Janet'd made it a point to hunt me out in the barn while I was saddling Gray. That there was one fine girl.

"I feel I should go with you while you are returning me to sanity, Mr. Williams," she said, "but right now my place is here. Daddy would worry terribly if I were not at home for the next few days. But I do appreciate it, and I wanted to thank you," she'd told me.

She had given me an odd little look and said, "Daddy likes you, you know. He seems to think quite highly of you. I guess . . . I guess that at first, when we just met, I was looking down on you, Stumpy."

I'd shrugged. "Most folks do, ma'am. I'm pretty well used to it."

"Well, if you wouldn't act so darn dumb and humble all the . . ." She had seemed sorta angry for some reason. "Never mind. I wanted to apologize. I have. So, thank you for helping us." She'd shoved her hand out like a man would for me to shake.

I don't know where in the world it came from, but I had a strange impulse that sent me right back to my cadet days attending receptions at the commandant's quarters. I popped to attention with a slap of leather boot heels, bowed over her hand, and brushed her knuckles with my lips. It had seemed to amuse her for she was smiling when I got on the old mule and rode west, toward Pueblo.

All during that ride I had kept thinking about the feel of her soft, slim fingers in my hand. And, worse, about the sweet, slender feel of her pressed against me when I'd found her in that cellar. I didn't even try to keep from thinking about it, and that was a bad sign.

I had to force my thoughts back in line when I got into town and checked back into the Grande.

It would not do to go relaxing now. The game was over for all practical purposes, but the other side might not know it yet. And there was still one Trask boy rambling around on the loose.

The desk clerk gave me the same room I'd had before, and when I saw that bed I decided Judge Hinsley could wait until morning to undo his part of the Trasks' mischief. It had been a long ride, and I had not slept well the night before. I opened a fast can of peaches from my duffel and went to bed right off, without even bothering to go down to dinner.

I woke to the sounds of early street traffic, feeling an awful lot better than when I'd gone to sleep. I also woke with a powerful hunger.

The dining room of the Grande was open for breakfast, I remembered, and that seemed a fine idea.

I brushed my town clothes into presentable condition and started to buckle my gunbelt in place since I'd taken to wearing it regular these days. Just in time I remembered the local ordinance on that subject and tucked the Remington into my waistband where it would be covered by my coat.

The dining room was a large, ornately appointed room that was a little dark for my taste at breakfast time. It was all dark reds and gold leaf and polished mahogany.

The lady who had charge of the dining room during the mornings let me pick a seat in a corner with walls behind me so I could see what was going on. I looked at the menu, which seemed to have been made up with Eastern visitors' tastes in mind, and asked could they improvise a little.

"Anything within reason, mister," she said with a smile that was doubly welcome on so hungry a morning.

"Sure am glad to hear that, ma'am. 'Cause what I could use is a big steak fried in tallow, a dish of stewed tomatoes, a stack of toasted bread with a bowl of flour gravy beside it, and about a quarter of one of your good pies. Deep-dish apple, if you have it."

"Coming right up," she said, and never hesitated nor let her smile slack the least bit. She walked away with a happy bounce in her step, and I thought it a fine idea to be greeted so pleasant of a morning.

Whoever was in the kitchen did a bang-up job in no more time than was necessary. And there was coffee in front of me right away.

I pitched into my food with a will and had it near about gone when another couple entered the dining room. It gave me something of a start at first, but then I decided what the heck. I stood just as polite as could be and invited them to join me.

"Mrs. Cates. Benny," I said as they were being seated. "You are looking well this morning."

Ben's expression was a trifle strained, but his mother had a calm and even pleasant look to her. Both were dressed to the teeth. Most respectable-looking folk I ever saw.

"Good morning, Stumpy," Ben said. "I believe you met my mother before."

"Well now, Benny, your late brother never introduced us proper, but you could say that we've met."

It produced an interesting reaction. Mrs. Cates got pale. Ben flushed hot red. "Not now, Ben," the woman said. "Not here."

"Very wise, ma'am," I assured her. "It would be so obvious. No way to avoid legal unpleasantness."

"Exactly," she said.

The waitress lady came, and they went back to being polite long enough to order light breakfasts. As soon as the happy lady had gone to the kitchen, though, the masks came off again.

"You push things, Williams. You really do," Ben said.

"Now isn't that silly of me," I told him. "An' all this time I'd been thinking it was y'all who was pushing me."

"You *have* been a nuisance, Mr. Williams," the woman said.

Ben said, "We do not approve of anyone interfering in our business."

"And very interesting business it was, too," I told them. "But I think you'd be better off now if you gave it up as a bad deal. Won't work now. Better light a shuck an' run while you can."

Ben got that haughty, superior look of his and sneered, "You're in way over your head, cowboy. You would never even begin to understand what we are doing."

"Prob'ly," I agreed with him. I smiled. "But I reckon Ezra Cates knows a few folks in the financial circles. An' me and my family have a few good friends who play that game. I'd guess you're going to have to capitalize awful heavy to put a corporation together. And I think maybe a few other friends can promise that you'll have to show your rolling stock and some firm contracts for steel purchase before any right of way is granted." It was childish, I know, but I was grinning from ear to ear.

I would say that the shot from Ezra Cates's bow found its mark. Both Ben and Mrs. Cates looked as if I'd just hit them betwixt the eyes with a hot branding iron.

"But all that stuff is away over my head," I said. Said it with malicious intent, I did. And I enjoyed it. Maybe Miss Janet was right. Maybe I should bait the tiger a little more regular. So all right, I'd go a step more.

"You know, Benny, you've just gotta learn, one of these days, that ol' Stumpy is a human person just the same as you. And maybe some brighter."

Oh, young Benjamin was purely seething. He leaned forward in his chair and looked to my waistline. When he saw no gunbelt there he reached with his right hand up under his coat toward his left side. He started to slide a stubby revolver out of there, but his mother laid a hand on his elbow.

"Not now, Ben. I told you that once." Her voice made it plain she wasn't to be crossed. Ben grunted and made the gun disappear again.

It was nice of him to show me where he carried the thing, I thought. "Temper, temper, Benny," I said, and stood up. "If you nice people will excuse me . . ." I left them glaring at my back and headed for the courthouse.

A nicely dressed boy told me the way to Judge Hinsley's cham-

bers. The judge was in when I got there and answered my knock
with the same deep "Come" I'd heard before.

He did not seem overjoyed to see me. "Ben Trask is in town
and in fine health," he said without preamble.

"Yes, I just had breakfast with him."

"So I noticed. I'd planned to breakfast at the Grande myself
this morning, but I lost my appetite when I got to the door."

"You should have joined us. You would have enjoyed watching
Ben squirm."

"Really?"

"Like a trout on a hook."

The old judge looked considerably more benign. "Tell me."

So I did, including Ezra Cates's pretty-well-confirmed ideas on
what the Trasks had been planning. When I was done Hinsley
leaned back in the swivel chair behind his desk. "Everything fits,
doesn't it, son?"

"I would say it does, judge. And I sure got a rise out of Ben and
Mrs. Cates during that breakfast you missed."

"Like a trout, I believe you said."

"Like a pair of them, Your Honor."

The old man chuckled. "And I can guess what you'll be wanting me to do now."

"Yes, sir. We need that order revoked. Do that and the Trasks
lose their one big club."

"You know, son, I don't believe I ever will want to know what
you would do if I went and refused to rescind that court order. I
believe that would blow a budding friendship all to hell and gone.
And I wouldn't want that."

I gave him a little thank-you by way of a nod of my head. "And
I would regret it just as much, believe me."

"Now then. We know where we are going. The question is how
to get there. Do you have a good lawyer?"

I smiled. "I think I know where I can engage the very best. If
you still offer counsel, that is."

"A diplomat as well, eh? Very good, son. I'll take the case." He
thought for just a few moments. "Simple, indeed. If you will cer-
tify to me that you have personally interviewed the young lady in

question and found her to be of sound mind, I can issue an order finding the original, ah, debility a temporary condition. The new order will declare the girl fully competent and capable of resuming responsibility for herself. The guardianship will of course be revoked." A laugh rumbled out of him. "If you like, son, I can insert a clause stipulating that in the event of a recurrence, you shall be appointed her guardian."

I blushed, I guess. Sure felt hot anyhow. "Don't know why you'd have thought of that."

"Surely you didn't think you were hiding anything? Not when you told me what all 'we' need to have done about this problem "

"Aw, there ain't nothing to try an' hide, Your Honor."

"Well, I won't bother trying to argue with you. Not worth the trouble by a long shot. You get out of here now and leave me to my legal chores cleaning up the mess I helped make. If you stop by the clerk's office this afternoon you can pick up a couple copies of my order. One for the girl and her father. And one you might want to give to Mrs. Cates."

I stood. "It is a shame I'm not a registered voter here. I sure would like a chance to vote for you, sir."

"Glad to hear that, son. Maybe you could find an excuse to make your home here. And make the both of us happy." He extended a big hand and said, "Take care of yourself now. Ben's not a boy to trust."

"Yes, sir. And thank you."

By the time I reached the door he had pulled a pair of wire-framed spectacles from his pocket and was bending over his desk. He was a likeable old scoundrel. And I just might have voted for him, given the chance.

CHAPTER 23

I had no desire to be sticking my head into any saloons or back alleys with Ben wandering around loose, so I took a side door out of the courthouse and found a little restaurant that had a big pot of strong coffee on the fire. The man running the place was a grease-spattered little fellow who didn't compare with the lady at the Grande for being friendly, but I could not complain much. The restaurant was small, running deep in a narrow building. What I liked was that it had few windows and thick walls.

I gave a boy a quarter and instructions to fetch me a fresh newspaper, and I was set for a good while with that and the coffee.

The morning passed quick enough, but there is only so much to read in a six-page newspaper. And drinking so much coffee makes it necessary to step outside after a while, so I decided not to trust the place for lunch. I paid my bill and headed back for the Grande, being sort of cautious about passing open doors and alleyways.

I thought about holing up in my room for the next few hours. I mean, I can do what I have to when it comes to facing a man, but why get into a shooting fight when maybe it can be avoided? The reason I finally decided to do my waiting in the lobby of the Grande was not so Ben could find me but so I'd be in a public place, in full view of witnesses.

From the way his mama had acted that morning it seemed the safest thing to do. So you might say it was a closer thing to cowardice than bravado that put me in an overstuffed armchair near the clerk's desk. Anyway, I am glad that's where I settled.

I was just getting into an article in an old *Police Gazette* about a trotting horse called Abe Downing, interesting story it was too, when I seen Ben and Mrs. Cates go by me into the dining room. Mrs. Cates gave me a sideways look going past, but Ben never blinked. Anyone watching would have thought he never noticed me setting there. I knowed better.

They had no sooner got out of sight than I got a fearful surprise. Miss Janet walked in, dressed pretty as a china doll in a long dress made of sateen or some such material of a shiny dark green color. The girl was pretty enough to take my breath away, but this was no time to be thinking of things such as that.

I jumped to my feet and had her by the elbow before I ever stopped to think how that might look.

"My word, Miss Janet. Don't you be going into that room. Ben Trask and his mother are in there, and I don't know what they might do if they saw you here."

She looked plenty startled, but she didn't ask any questions. "All right," she said, and slid an inch or two closer to me. It was an unthinking reaction, I knew, but I did not mind that in the least. It seemed she was more willing than she'd once been to accept my judgment of things.

"I think the best thing would be to tuck you away out of sight for a few hours," I said.

"All right."

The next question was where. "Do you know anyone in town you could stay with for that time?" She shook her head no.

I sure didn't know anybody, save for Judge Hinsley. And he was busy at the courthouse today. No matter how much I tried to think in those few seconds, I only came up with one answer. Maybe there was some unwanted streak in me that wanted it that way.

I could feel my face getting hot again, and I guess I looked something akin to a beet with beard stubble. "Ma'am, the only place I could think of would be . . . my room upstairs." I said the last words in a low, embarrassed rush.

But she never reacted at all. "All right, Stumpy."

I edged her away from the dining-room door, wary lest Ben come out of it and see us, and led her up the stairs.

At least with Ben safely occupied at lunch I didn't have to

worry about us being jumped in the hallway. I unlocked the door to my room and let her in, then made sure it was properly locked behind me. Miss Janet gave no reaction to the fact that this was some strange man's room. She seated herself in one of the needle-point chairs and put the situation a little more right by motioning me to the matching chair on the other side of the tea table. "Please sit down, Stumpy."

"Yes, ma'am." I started to throw my hat on the big bed, then thought better of that and carried it over to the dressing table on the other side of the room.

"Have you talked with the judge?" she asked.

"Yes, ma'am," I said. I perched on the chair across from her and tried to get rid of the discomfort I felt. But this really was not right, and I did not want Miss Janet's reputation to suffer. She had troubles enough without me causing more.

"Judge Hinsley is fixing up the legal papers now to change what Ben had done. He said the papers'll be ready this afternoon, all filed as official court documents and some copies I can pick up. One copy for you an' your daddy. Another for Ben and his mother."

"It seems to be over then, doesn't it?"

"Almost, ma'am, but not quite. For one thing, Ben and Mrs., uh, his mother, don't know yet how completely it is ended. And for another, Ben strikes me as the kind of ol' boy who might turn nasty when he finds out the fairy dream is over an' he has to wake up now."

"Then you think he might still try to hurt Dad?"

"Yes, ma'am. Or you. I just couldn't say for sure."

Her eyes were large. "He might try to take it out on you too, Stumpy."

"That would be the best choice of the three," I said.

"I couldn't bear that, Stumpy." Her voice was sweet, and she was genuinely concerned this time. Not just being polite. It got my pulse to thumping even though I knew perfectly well how she meant it.

But she had accepted me as a friend, I thought. She was thinking of me as a person, not as some half-wit hindrance. I was awful pleased about that.

She shifted in her chair, and I wondered was she having some worries about being in this hotel room with me. She brightened and asked, "Tell me about yourself, Stumpy. You already know practically everything about me, so it is only fair of you to return the favor."

"Yes, ma'am," I said.

And I guess I did what she asked. It got easier as I talked. Some, anyway. I don't guess I've ever sat down and talked so much about myself, not even to Lawyer Farley back in Apishapa City.

I told her about it all. The hard times following the war when I was helping to put a stock operation together. The good times at school later. And the grown-up times since, trying to run the place for Mama and the girls and their husbands.

I guess I even let down and complained some about those boys. But I'd been sorta disappointed a long time by them and hadn't expected to be. I'd expected them to take charge some when they come into the family. It isn't like they were strangers to the business, them growing up in it the same as me except for having more education when they were of an age for it.

I don't guess I'd ever told that to a solitary soul before, but I did to Miss Janet. Of course I knew she was too kindhearted to be seen looking down on me for such feelings. She wouldn't go repeating it anywhere. And it was awful nice to be talking with her, knowing she would be that way about anything I said.

It was a temptation to tell her more. To tell her how high I regarded her, for instance. But that would be going maybe too far. I didn't want to lay a burden on her that would make her uncomfortable when I was around, so I held my peace on that subject anyway.

When my spring was all the way unwound and I finally shut up, she smiled at me. "Do you mind if I say something?" she asked.

"No, ma'am. I don't reckon I would mind anything you might say."

"Good. Stumpy Williams, I think you are a very nice man." She giggled and saved me from whatever my reaction might have been. "And I have a very embarrassing question to ask you."

"Yes, ma'am?"

"Well . . . I'm sorry, Stumpy, but I have forgotten what you told me your real first name is."

I was relieved to find out that's all it was. "It's James, ma'am. James Denton Williams, soon to be of Utah."

"Of course. Thank you. It was stupid of me to have forgotten."

"Oh no, ma'am. No reason you should remember a thing like that."

"There is every reason. Anyway, it will not happen again. Would you mind if I were to call you Jim?"

"Why, no, ma'am. I wouldn't mind at all. Though it's been a lot of years since anybody called me that. Even Mama calls me Stumpy now."

"Fine, Jim. And in return I would like you to make me a promise. All right?"

"Yes, ma'am. Just name it."

"Jim, I want you to promise me that never, under any circumstances whatever, will you ever again call me 'ma'am.' I am NOT the same age as your mother, and you shouldn't refer to me as you would to one of her contemporaries."

"Why, I'd be happy to do that, Miss Janet," I said.

"Just Janet, please."

"Yes, m . . . Yes, Janet."

She nodded her head and seemed satisfied with that idea.

I got up and looked out the window to the street below. There was nothing much going on, just a regular flow of wagons and buggies and a few heavy drays with their drafters plopping huge hooves in the dust. From the slant of the sun I figured we had wasted enough time, and the papers should be ready.

"The clerk should have everything we need now," I told the girl. I hesitated. "You could stay here, but I hate to leave you alone here. If Ben came calling for me . . . well, it wouldn't be a good idea, that's all."

"I can walk with you." She fetched up her purse and was ready.

"This whole thing *does* concern me, Jim. That is the reason Daddy agreed to let me come into town. As soon as those papers are ready, I want to make sure the sheriff gets the whole story, straight from me."

"Yes, ma'am." She faked a quick pout, and I amended that. "Yes, Janet."

I slipped the Remington from my waistband and had it ready in my hand before I eased the door open. Ben could of been waiting in the hallway. I checked the corridor carefully before I put the gun away and collected Miss Janet. I escorted her down to the public—and much safer—lobby.

"Smile now, girl. Things are looking up." She did.

The court clerk remembered me and was just as cordial as he'd been before.

Yes, sir, Judge Hinsley left instructions that two copies of the order were to be delivered to J. D. Williams. Yes, sir, the copies were ready, certified as true copies by the clerk and authenticated with the official seal. No, sir, there was no charge for the service.

The clerk smiled at Miss Janet, much nicer even than he'd smiled at me, and handed them over.

Such ordinary-looking, such very important papers.

I read one over quickly, fearful all of a sudden that the judge just might have carried through on his joke and put me down as some sort of standby guardian, but he had not, thank goodness.

Miss Janet read over the other copy, and it was easy to see the happiness that was in her eyes. "Thank you, Jim," she said, and right there in the clerk's office of the county courthouse she raised up and give me a kiss on the cheek. She was so tiny she had to get up on tiptoe to do it. The touch of her lips was light as the down on a new-hatched chick, but the impact was a lot more than that.

"You do blush easily, don't you?" she said mischievously.

"Yes, ma'am," I said. "We'd better go see the sheriff now."

I asked the clerk, who was grinning more than he ought, and he said the sheriff shared the jail with the city police and we could find his office in the next block. I thanked him and got Miss Janet out of there.

I guess my thoughts were not entirely where they ought to have been either. I took Miss Janet down the stone steps and across the front courthouse lawn in the most direct path to the sheriff's office. We were about to step off the wood-planked sidewalk to cross the street when I heard a commotion behind.

I never will know how it was that I realized what was happening, but I flung a shoulder into Miss Janet and knocked her in a sprawl of skirts into the dirt of the street. There was no cover near us save a scant four inches or so of lip between the sidewalk and the street level.

I felt something like a baseball bat smash into my back, then heard the dull report of a revolver.

The impact spun me around toward the right, and I tripped over Miss Janet and went down before I could claw the Remington out from under my coat.

I was half on top of the girl and rolled free of her so his next shot would not be so likely to hit her.

Ben shot again, and I felt splinters gouge into my face from where they'd splashed off of the sidewalk.

I had my gun out now and for the first time got a look at Ben. He looked like a crazy man. His hat was knocked off and his coat was pulled askew. There was some fellow laying on the ground beside him, bleeding from a slash over the ear.

Ben was standing at an angle to me like he was on a target range. He cocked the big-caliber bulldog revolver he'd carried in the shoulder holster and brought it down on me.

I let fly with my first shot before him. The bullet took him high in the right side, the one facing me. I guess he flinched. His bulldog fired, and the bullet went high, somewhere away over my head. I could hear it go past like an angry five-pound bumblebee.

I fired again into his body, then shifted my aim higher. The third bullet hit him in the neck and snapped his head around.

Ben staggered and went down, forward on his face. I wasn't taking any chances. I took careful aim and shot him twice more and would of kept on shooting except my gun was empty.

I looked quick to the side. Miss Janet was all right. She was laying in the dirt beside me, right smack beside me. I'd thought she was a good eight or ten feet away.

"Now I've gone an' got your pretty dress dirty, ma'am. I'm sorry."

Saying that was the last thing I remembered for some time.

CHAPTER 24

"Quit being so balky. Eat what I give you and be glad of it."
The deep voice was unmistakable. Judge Hinsley had me propped
up and was forcing a spoonful of some sticky liquid into my
mouth.

I went to open my eyes and discovered the darn things were already open. I just hadn't realized it at first. I got everything back
toward normal and looked at him. His meaty jowls spread into a
broad smile.

"I take it you're back to stay?" he asked. I managed a weak nod
and identified the taste of the sticky stuff at the same time.
Chicken stock. It must have been powerful thick.

"There was some doubt about it, you know," Hinsley said. "In-
fection of some sort. Glad you decided to throw it. I might have
been stuck with the shipping charges. Besides, we wouldn't have
known whether to send you to Texas or to Utah. A touchy point,
that, if you think about it."

"Yeah," I said. I could hardly hear the word myself. I don't
know if he heard it or had to watch for lip movement. Which-
ever, the response seemed to please him all out of proportion to
the accomplishment.

"That little Cates girl will be pleased," he said while he was
pushing some more stock into me. "Poor thing's about worn out.
She's been dashing back and forth between here and her daddy's
ranch, trying to mend the both of you at once and you two lying
in beds forty miles apart."

I raised an eyebrow.

"Where is she now?"

I shook my head.

"When is she coming back?" Another shake.

"Where are you now? Is that what you're asking?" A nod. "You're cluttering up my spare bedroom, that's where. And the girl should be back early tomorrow afternoon if her papa is all right. The last report had him improving quite nicely."

He injected another dose of chicken stock. "No questions about Ben and his mother?" I nodded.

"I thought so. As you should very well know, Benjamin is now best known for the quality of the stonework marking his grave. His mother is another story.

"The sheriff and I had a lengthy consultation on that subject. Not a dang thing we could expect to prove if we had been foolish enough to charge her with anything. As far as the law is concerned, the woman was clean as new-driven snow and all that nonsense. However, I was generous enough to provide Ez Cates with a quick, quiet annulment. So the marriage never happened. A bit after the fact, but one does what one can," he said with a grimace.

He kept on talking, but his voice was faint and soon was not there at all. I blinked hard to try and get my vision back, and Miss Janet was there. They told me a whole day had passed, but I'd missed it. I was not aware of the passage of any time at all.

As soon as I wakened Miss Janet grabbed a cup of some other variety of broth. She wielded her spoon with a solicitous air and a wide, seemingly even tender smile on her face.

Judge Hinsley leaned forward. I hadn't noticed him before, but he was sitting right next to Miss Janet.

Between them they finished telling me what all I'd missed the past eight days. There had been an inquest, and Ben's death was ruled justifiable homicide by reason of self-defense. The man Ben had slugged had made that clear. Poor fellow had tried to stop Ben from shooting, without notable success.

Apparently the county sheriff had been right insistent about charging me with something at first. He hadn't much liked the idea of me shooting at poor Benny when he was down.

It was sort of funny listening to Hinsley and Miss Janet each trying to give the other all the credit for dissuading him from that notion. They seemed to be forming a real mutual admiration team.

After a few minutes the judge got up and excused himself. He winked at me as he left.

Miss Janet pulled her chair closer to the bed. "You look better, Jim."

I whispered, "You look perfect."

She blushed. "I guess you must still be delirious."

"Still?"

She got much, much redder though I would not have thought that possible. "Yes. You . . . did talk a good bit."

Now I got some red my own self. "What'd I say?"

"Well, you were very . . . complimentary."

"Lordy, I sure am sorry, ma'am."

"Don't be," she said quickly. "It was really, well, flattering. And most unexpected."

I wanted to turn my face to the wall and pass out or go to sleep or something, but I couldn't.

"Jim?"

"Yes, ma'am?"

She looked stern for a moment. "You promised, remember?"

"Yes. Janet."

"There is something I want to talk with you about, Jim. I know you are a fine stockman." She held her hand up. "Don't interrupt. You *are* a very fine stockman. I know it. And you are a very responsible person. But you have buried yourself in your family for the last fifteen years or more. Well, I've been thinking about what you said about your brothers-in-law. Could it be that you haven't given them a chance to help run the ranch? Could you have handled things so completely that there was nothing they could do without being afraid of stepping on your toes?"

There was an obvious, easy answer to that, but . . . "I really don't know, Janet," I said after I'd had a moment to think about it. "I suppose . . . it *might* be possible. I don't know."

"All right. Think about it. And when you do, think about this too. In a few days Daddy will be well enough to be brought into town. He wants to do it right away so he can see you. When he does, he wants to thank you, of course.

H 2

"He also wants to ask if you would take over operation of the Rocker EC. That's our ranch. He doesn't know about your family's new ranch in Utah." Her eyes were bright, and she was becoming excited. "Oh, Jim, let your family take care of themselves now. This is the perfect opportunity for them to do that. And for you. No one will be set in the old patterns in Utah. There is no need for them to be. Let them make their own way, set their own patterns, work for *their* families.

"And you," she blushed again. "You could stay here, and . . . I'd like for you to, Jim."

I closed my eyes so I wouldn't have to look at her when I said it. "Miss Janet, ma'am. Maybe I should leave the boys go their own way. It sounds like a right thing to do, though it will take some thinking.

"But Miss Janet, about staying here to help you and your daddy. I . . . would like to do that maybe more than you'll ever know. But, ma'am, I don't know that I could spend so much time around . . . well, around you, ma'am. You see, I got feelings the same as anybody else, and you are a truly beautiful girl. And, lordy, Miss Janet, I wouldn't want to do anything in this world to hurt you or embarrass you or to make you feel uncomfortable about having me around. I mean . . ."

"Dammit, James Williams, look at me."

I did, startled by her sharp outburst.

"Don't you think I know that, Jim?"

"But . . ."

"Shut up and hold me." Of a sudden she was off her chair and bent close over me. "We'll practice more later, but this will do for now," she murmured.

The whole world was shut out by her long, perfect hair falling around my face. There was only that. And her eyes, a blue so dark and true they were almost black. And the delicate, clean girl-scent of her. And the soft, sweet taste of her lips.

I reckoned I had come home, and not to Utah like I'd expected. I didn't mind the change in plans. Nor the way my eyes were so misty with a sudden wetness. It was perfectly all right.

Perfectly.